THE TIMELESS ZODIAC

Book II

The Timeless Zodiac
Book II

Written by
Dana Skvarek II

Cover and Illustrations by
Jolene Skvarek

Edited by
Jeff Goeson

2018

Second Edition: 2018

ISBN 978-1-387-88070-6

Vivifica Studios, LLC
4381 North 75th St, Suite 201
Scottsdale, AZ 85251

www.VivificaStudios.com

Dedication

To those whom the Chaotic One would steal from.
Remember.

Chapter 1

Paris was no more.

The Eiffel Tower was torn from its base and shredded into pieces by the claws of the Dark Ones. The Louvre was ransacked and its art and history burned and lost forever. The Arch de Triumph became a ruin and the place of resurrection for a dark and sinister force, whose bones had laid in the catacombs beneath the city for centuries. The Chaos had begun, yet again, in this modern age.

A thin, tall figure, wrapped in torn and bloodied black robes strolled among the destruction. Minutes ago, he sent the bulk of his forces across space and time to the West coast of the United States, where they would wreak even more havoc. Now, the skeletal Wicked Man walked in the rubble of the former City of Light and admired his handiwork.

"Despair, all you who live," he smiled and growled. "Despair, you who flourish across the Earth. Wail and mourn for your lost cities, your great accomplishments. When the sun sets, you will remember them, no more."

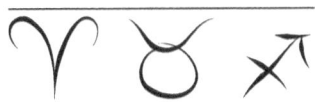

The city of San Francisco was under siege, and the first of the twelve stewards, accompanied by the Zodiac that called them, had taken up positions across the city. Samantha, The Healer, imbued by a crafty trick that made her countenance appear angelic and sporting the Armband of Cleopatra, hovered a few meters above ground by the Golden Gate Bridge. The Timeless One, Aries the Ram, held her up by the waist to keep up the appearance of being an otherworldly messenger.

"Please hurry, there isn't much time! Cross the bridge. Leave anything that can be replaced. Save your lives, your loved ones. Hurry," she insisted of the growing throng. Some stopped to take video and pictures as they escaped the Chaos taking place nearby.

"You are doing an excellent job, Healer," Aries whispered from behind Samantha.

"Remind me to punch Jude for his little angel trick," she said over shoulder.

"His angel trick may be the one thing that encouraged the people to listen."

"He still could have told me," Samantha said under her breath. "Please, hurry!"

Riku Yatsukura, The Warrior, was not having as much luck in the underground BART system. His initial contact with the people of San Francisco didn't bear much fruit, as no one understood Japanese. So, Riku resorted to much less subtle methods of clearing people out.

"No, you listen! Me, Godzilla! You need run!" he stammered in his best attempt to speak English to the crowd of San Francisco's finest, that had now surrounded him with tasers and batons drawn. Riku held out in front of him the very old, very elegant, and very sharp Sword of Achilles. He sung it back and forth as the police force drew nearer and nearer.

"You not understand! Disaster come!"

"Just calm down, Godzilla," one of the police said as he inched closer. "Put your sword down and we can talk about the disaster."

"You all in danger! Please run! I try help!" Riku begged of them as the group closed in on him.

Just then he turned his eyes to the top of the steps to see a monstrous face looking down at them all. One of the Dark Ones, a wolf-beast with the face of a man, snarled at the group. Its fangs dripped with saliva and its low growls echoed and amplified in the underground tunnels. The police slowly turned their heads towards the new threat.

"What in the hell?..." one officer commented.

Riku fixed his gaze on the monster and defiantly strode through the circle of cops to take point.

"Hey demon," he shouted in Japanese, "I'm The Warrior, come and get me!"

The Dark One, now joined by two others, barreled down the steps towards their prey. With a loud shout and a few well planned steps, Riku sliced the head clean off the first, twisted and cut the second in half, then planted his sword into the skull of the last one.

He pulled the blade from the beast, flung black tar-like blood onto one of the officers, and replaced his sword in his belt. For a few long, pulse pounding heartbeats, the officers stood motionless. Then the first officer, the one that spoke to Riku, trembling, grabbed his radio.

"Dispatch we need a full evac of the BART tunnels, priority one."

Riku smiled, bowed low to the police, and turned to ascend the steps.

Jude, the man chosen to be The Prophet, had set up a flawless plan to thwart the coming of their evil adversary. Having seen in a vision the destruction of San Francisco, he concluded that if the three stewards, aided by the Zodiac, were to advance on the city first, they could prevent the disastrous vision of his from coming to pass.

He gave the orders to Riku, jotted a few words in his notebook and thus granted the angelic appearance to Samantha, then positioned himself and the Timeless One, Taurus the Bull, at the foot of the Transamerica Building. He knew if they all played their parts, nothing could stop them from saving the city.

He was magnificently mistaken.

While Taurus, clad in his golden armor and armed with his mighty lance, fought off wave after wave of advancing Dark Ones, Jude scribbled notes in his notebook in attempt to change the outcome of things. But it wasn't working. He turned his eyes upward and watched in horror as the top floors of the Transamerica pyramid suddenly burst into the flame.

"Prophet!" Taurus shouted, as he abandoned his brawl and was upon Jude in two great steps. The Zodiac held up his lance and an invisible umbrella of energy covered the two of them, just as glass and steel rained down from above. Jude stared at the debris that crashed down all around them and watched the flames atop the building rise. Then he heard the laughter.

"What pitiless hope have you filled their heads with, Zodiac?" Jude looked and saw a cloud of smoke moving towards them from down the street. It almost looked as though blackened, burnt hands were reaching out from the cloud, grasping at nothing but propelling the whole thing forward.

"You feed them pretty little lies to follow, based on ignorance, while I bring them truth."

"Apollyon," Taurus growled.

"Taurus. Such a pleasure to see you again," the voice from the cloud said. It stopped moving a few meters away from Jude. The Darkness began to fold in on itself, like the smoke of a cigarette being pulled back into the mouth of the smoker. It compacted and coalesced into the shape of a person, then features began to form. Fingers, ears, even hair formed out of the smoke until there stood before them the Chaotic One, the Destroyer, Apollyon.

"What did you hope to achieve, I wonder?" Apollyon teased. "Save the people, save the day? Hm? Did you believe my return into this wretched world could be delayed if you wrote in your little book?" He laughed.

"I...we won't let you destroy this city," Jude said, in a voice just above a whisper.

"What was that, boy? I didn't hear you."

"I said...we won't let you...destroy this city." He repeated a little louder.

"Now that's the spirit. Let's hear it again, hm? Louder, with more feeling this time."

"We won't let you..."

Jude was cut off abruptly as Apollyon swung his hand through the air. Though meters away the force was enough to create a backhand effect that knocked Jude clean off his feet.

"You won't let me what?! Say it again! Again!" Apollyon crouched down low near Jude's face, all the while Taurus stood there and frowned.

"We...won't..."

Apollyon gently palmed Jude's head and started pushing it down into the asphalt.

"Repeat after me, *Prophet!* We, will, *not…*" Apollyon mocked, barely containing his glee. Jude grimaced in pain, his eyes looking to Taurus who stood unmoving.

"Taurus…help…please…"

"That's not what I said!" Apollyon shouted, lifting Jude's head and crashing it back down onto the asphalt.

Jude's eyes went fuzzy, and he could taste blood in his mouth. This was a bad idea, this whole thing was a bad idea. To think that he could go against a cosmic being who, for centuries, has laid waste to civilization after civilization.

"Now, I said, repeat after…"

Apollyon paused, his eyebrow lowering and he looked over to his side. The small hand of a woman gripped his arm.

"Let…him…go."

Apollyon looked up at the golden image of Samantha, still glowing from Jude's magic words written about her. The Armband of Cleopatra shown with an even brighter light on her bicep as she squeezed harder.

"Well, if it isn't the little Healer as well," Apollyon grinned. "My dear, why don't you give me a minute and I'll be right with…"

Samantha had had enough.

She grit her teeth and flung Apollyon across the street as though he were no more than a rag doll. The great creature crashed into a doughnut shop, shattering glass and metal.

"We need to leave," Aries suddenly appeared next to Taurus, who quickly shook out of his statued state and picked up Jude in an instant.

"The city is lost, let us go." Taurus said, and just like that he was gone.

Samantha lingered a moment and stared into the hole in the building across the street. From deep inside she could hear the laughter of Apollyon. It grew louder, echoed, even carried down the street. Soon car alarms began blaring and windows shattered nearby as it grew louder and louder. Great, long wisps of smoke began to shoot out from the darkness, wrapping around nearby street lamps and support columns.

"Healer, we must leave now!" Aries urged. Samantha, eyes still locked on the doughnut shop, nodded her head and grabbed Aries by the arm. The next moment they were gone.

Chapter 2

The air was very cool and quite crisp in the northern town of Hammerfest, Norway. As with most days in April, the temperature wouldn't climb past 2° celsius today, even with the sun shining bright and very few clouds in the sky. The permafrost clung to various parts of the ground like it always did here, but surprisingly there were patches of thick, green grass scattered about.

On one such patch stood two eternal beings, one whom was stalking his latest prey, the newest steward to be added into the fold, and the other who hadn't set foot on the Earth for centuries.

The cool air between them was then split with such speed and force that the resulting vacuum left in the wake of the swinging object would reverberate and crash like thunder. The Timeless One, Leo the Lion, arced his cudgel across the air, the flanges on the end expanding and growing three times their normal size. The enlarged end of the cudgel came within millimeters of striking Aquarius the Water Bearer, across the face, and would have, had he not dodged with a supernatural speed.

"Honestly, Leo," Aquarius said, "must we do this? It is a tremendous waste of time after all."

"Time? Waste of time?" Leo said, incredulous. "We are timeless beings, *brother*. The only time being wasted is mine, listening to your lip!" Leo swung the weapon again, the force

of which spun his whole body around in a circle but allowed for him to attempt another strike.

Aquarius dodged just as easily as before.

"You are causing quite a racket, you know. The humans have heard that noise, no doubt, and will come seeking its source."

"Let them come! Makes my job easier finding my steward. 'Course you wouldn't know about that, since you left your charge…
how many ages ago?" Leo swung again, this time striking the ground and tossing mud and grass into the air.

"That is why I am here, you oaf," Aquarius suddenly moved like lightning and was upon Leo, one hand on his lapel and the other gripping his wrist, preventing Leo from raising his weapon again.

"I'm trying to help. To prevent the Chaos."

"Where were you," Leo stared intently into the other's eyes, "when Yggdrasil fell? Where were you when the Hanging Gardens burned? Did you watch from way out in outer space while the Wicked Man was dug up, or were you too busy?"

Aquarius heaved a heavy sigh, and let Leo go.

"I am here now. For all my past transgressions, I beg your forgiveness." He bowed his head and clasped his hands held out towards. Leo. Leo retracted his cudgel and placed it back on his hip.

"Don't beg my forgiveness. Beg it from the honored dead, whose screams I still hear. Whose names are long forgotten, whose very memory was blotted out by Apollyon. Beg your forgiveness from them. I have work to do."

"Let me earn my place back again. I can help. I know the location of the Cistern. You seek The Purifier. What could he…"

"It's a she, in this age." Leo quickly corrected.

"What could *she* possibly do to help without the Cistern?"

"You tell me. In the last age Gemini was charged with finding The Purifier. And when they did, he worked until his very last breath to cleanse the Chaos. He even restored The Prophet's memories while his own life bled away. Did you see that, from way out in the stars?"

"Please, if you only could understand…"

"Then make me understand. Tell me what was so important that you hid an artifact and fled your charge? Hmmm?"

Aquarius paused. He tried to open his mouth but knew the words would not come out. *Could* not come out.

"I…cannot say." He slouched where he stood.

Leo turned from Aquarius and began walking towards the town. Aquarius straightened up and watched his brother walk away, unsure of exactly what to do.

"With all twelve pieces, they have a chance you know."

Leo stopped and looked over his shoulder.

"They've always had a chance. Perhaps you forgot that too."

Aquarius hung his head as Leo vanished from the area.

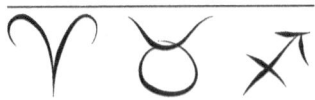

The dirt and leaves of the Redwood National Forest stirred and burst from its rest as Taurus and an injured Jude suddenly appeared amidst the great trees. Taurus lay Jude on the ground on his back, and pressed a larger than average hand against his forehead. One eye was bruised, and there was swelling on the side of his face that had been pummeled into the asphalt. There were abrasions on his temple and dried blood in his hair as well.

If not for the quick action of Samantha, and Taurus pulling Jude out of the situation, he likely would not be alive. Bruises, cuts, and swelling were among the least he would have faced had he spent another minute at the hands of Apollyon.

The sticks and leaves rustled again and there appeared Aries with Samantha, no longer glowing, in tow.

"Where is he? I'm gonna kill him!" Samantha spun in circles looking for Jude.

"It is yours to heal," Taurus looked up at her, drawing her attention, "not to kill. Observe." Taurus pointed down to Jude who lay sprawled on the dirt, unconscious.

"Well...okay. I'll heal him. *Then* I'll kill him." Samantha said as she knelt down next to Jude. "How do I..."

"How would you?" Taurus asked.

Samantha began her normal routine and checked her patient's breathing, pulse, and rolled him carefully into a more manageable position on his back. Jude was breathing, but unresponsive to everything else she tried. Without her kit, she was at a loss of how exactly she could help him. Then it dawned on her.

"Oh," she looked at her arm and remembered the Armband. Samantha placed her hand against Jude's head and closed her eyes. She tried to imagine what he looked like before, but all she saw was his stupid face. She cleared her throat and took a deep breath, then focused on his words. Jude had tried to save everyone with his plan, and even somehow managed to affect the way others viewed her.

Just as before, she felt a strange heat moving beneath and all around her hand. Even with her eyes closed, Samantha could almost see Jude's cuts closing, the swelling receding, and the bruise returning to the normal color of his stupid face.

Behind her, Aries glanced at Taurus, who was also watching, and smiled at her steward.

Jude's eyes suddenly shot open and he sat up fast, just barely missing Samantha's nose with his forehead. He coughed and looked around left and right frantically, as though expecting to hear the laughter of the Destroyer.

"Where are we!? Where is he?!" Jude tried to stand but tumbled back.

"We are far from his reach. Calm yourself Prophet," Taurus moved forward and placed a hand on Jude, bringing him to a complete calm with a touch. "We are four hundred and eighty kilometers north of San Francisco. What you call the 'Redwood Forest'."

"Are we the only ones here?" Samantha asked, as she brushed the leaves off her pants.

"There are others nearby, but not within earshot," Aries said.

"Where's Riku? Did he make it?" Jude looked up at Taurus.

"He will be here…"

The leaves exploded and Riku popped into the clearing, Sagittarius right behind him atop his steed.

"San Francisco has fallen," Sagittarius announced. "The Warrior did much to rid the streets of the Dark Ones and allowed many innocents to flee. But alas, the city has been taken by Apollyon."

"Did you guys see? I cut them right in half with this beautiful beautiful Viking sword!" Riku excitedly kissed the blade, and let out a somewhat crazy laugh. "Never again! I will never again ridicule Vikings! That was awesome!" He looked over at the faces of his comrades, whose expressions were less than jubilant.

"That's good, Riku. I'm glad at least some people were saved," Samantha turned to give Jude a look.

"What happened with you guys? Did it all work?"

"No," Jude grunted as he leaned against a tree. "I failed pretty miserably. And Apollyon hammered my face into the ground. Literally. Speaking of that," Jude turned to face Taurus. "What the hell, man!? You just stood there!"

Taurus gave a slight bow.

"We told you, we Zodiac are forbidden from directly interfering with Apollyon. Once he is present, we are but watchers."

"Yeah well that's pretty convenient. I'm getting my face smashed into the street and you're watching. Thanks. Thanks a lot."

"But, we saved people. People lived. Doesn't that mean we won?" Riku smiled, trying to bring a silver lining to the moment.

"Unfortunately no," Aries looked down on the little Japanese teen. "Apollyon will erase even the memory of that city from the Earth. Those that survived, that fled, will know only that they have lost their homes. But they will lack the knowledge of where they came from to begin with."

Samantha shook her head. "So now what do we do?"

"The world is far more connected than in ages past," Sagittarius moved forward as he spoke. "Only one other age has ever known the scope of the world, and it was long erased. Apollyon will continue his campaign of destruction until every major city, every civilization that exists today, is no more."

Those sobering words struck hard at the three stewards, and all of them became silent for a time. Riku sat down on his knees and closed his eyes to meditate, while Samantha sat back against a giant redwood and Jude paced. A half hour passed before Jude, rubbing his hands through his hair, finally started off into the forest.

"Prophet?" Taurus called after him.

"I...I just need a few minutes, okay?" Jude said without looking back. He marched quickly into the forest and weaved through the large trunks to avoid being seen.

The moment he was fairly certain he had escaped their view, Jude broke down sobbing. Watching the aftermath of Paris was one thing, but seeing the Dark Ones attack and tear at the city of San Francisco, and watching the debris fall from overhead right towards him, and being personally attacked by some cosmic villain...it was all, already, too much. He collapsed next to a tree and curled into a ball, burying his face against his knees while the tears flowed.

Sure, they had saved hundreds, maybe even thousands of people, and sure they had survived to live and fight another day. But this was nothing like what he imagined. Everything had happened so fast, and was so chaotic, that Jude didn't have time enough to think and plan ahead. His little experiment with Samantha apparently had paid off, but when it came right down to split-second decisions, what he wrote in his notebook was far too little, and much too late.

Then Jude heard the unmistakable sound of crushing leaves and sticks, as someone was walking in his direction. He jumped to his feet and wiped his eyes on the sleeve of his shirt. He didn't want Riku or Samantha to see him like this, and was prepared to tell off whoever it was, when he was met with a surprise.

"Well hello there, Prophet," Aquarius said.

Chapter 3

Jude quickly looked the Zodiac up and down, and although a little confused, he instantly remembered him from the vision of Atlantis that Taurus had shown him. Before him stood the curly haired, kind face of Aquarius.

"You do not know me, but I am…"

"Aquarius," Jude cut him off. "I know who you are."

Aquarius was visibly shocked and cleared his throat before continuing.

"Ah, well allow me to introduce myself, then, if only as a formality. I am Aquarius, the Water Bearer, one of the Timeless Zodiac."

Aquarius crossed one arm over his stomach and made a low bow before Jude, who was somewhat unimpressed.

"Yeah, it's uh, nice to meet you." Jude said, trying to be polite. "So, you're here to help?"

Aquarius straightened back up and smiled down at Jude.

"One aspect I always enjoyed of humanity, was their ability to get right to the point. No need for small talk or, beating around the bush, as some would say."

"That happens when we have a shelf life. I'm not gonna live forever. So, you're here to help?"

"I am," Aquarius answered, while trying to hide his discomfort with the situation. "Tell me, how is it you know who I am? You instantly recognized me, and I must say, I'm very curious."

"Taurus showed me your failure in Atlantis," Jude said bluntly. After the recent loss, he wasn't in much of a mood for chit chat, and was very eager to know why, after everything Taurus had told him, would Aquarius decide only now to return to the mix.

"I see. Yes, it is the duty of The Prophet to catalog the things that have come before. I myself have trained a few Prophets in ages past."

"But not in a long time. Not since you failed Atlantis and ran away. Right?" Aquarius pursed his lips and forced a smile. Would it be so bad to stomp this one into the ground? Would they really miss him? There would always be another Prophet in another age...

"Quite right. My shortcomings..."

"Failure."

"...in Atlantis were regrettable," Aquarius said, his patience with this one already running thin. "However, I never stopped watching, even if from afar, the stories humanity wove. And now and then, someone would truly catch my eye, as you have, Jude."

Jude was instantly taken aback by the reference to his name, and not his title, so much so that his hard defensive shell wavered a moment.

"Oh, uh, thanks. I guess."

Aquarius curtly smiled. This was the opening he was looking for.

"As I said, we Zodiac can see impossible distances, and something you have done surprised me. I highly doubt Taurus has told you, but you have already accomplished something no other Prophet has ever even attempted."

"Well I tried to, ya know, do my best and all. We still lost in San Francisco, but I think if we keep working together as a team and…" Jude trailed off. "What exactly did I do?"

"You changed things," Aquarius said softly as he knelt one knee on the forest floor. He now looked up, barely, at Jude. "The Warrior has his Sword, and the Healer has her Armband. The Guardian, whom you'll meet soon enough, has Leo's Golden Fleece, and so on and so forth. But you, Jude, you have your Tome. Be it a chisel and tablet, or pen and paper, or memory itself. And that is more powerful than you can imagine."

Jude's shoulders suddenly stopped slouching, and the distraught look of disappointment that had been painted on his face suddenly washed away. Here was a glimmer of hope that they might still be able to win, and by his own hand no less.

"But," he started, "I tried to change things during the fight. It wouldn't work."

"Ah yes, when an action is already set, already in motion, it is written, so to speak. But *before* the action, that is when you can manipulate the very fabric of time around you and mold the outcome how you see fit." Aquarius put a hand on Jude's shoulder. "And this is why I have come to pay you a visit. You see, I am in need of *your* help."

Jude was sold. He had just learned that his power could rival those of his comrades, and now here was a Timeless One seeking his help. His own failure in San Francisco would be wiped clean, and he would be heralded as the savior of civilization itself. Maybe even given his own private island to host D&D parties with his friends…Why not?

"There is an artifact," Aquarius said, shaking Jude from his day dream. "One of my own creation, bestowed upon mankind very long ago. Unfortunately it has been…lost to the rest of us. Even now, Leo seeks it for The Purifier, but he will never find it without aid."

"My help?"

"Exactly," Aquarius smiled. "You can direct Leo to the proper place, and once there he will lead The Purifier, your next ally, to the Cistern."

"You aren't taking the...the Purifier there yourself?" Jude asked. Aquarius stood up again, his height made Jude crane his neck to look at the Zodiac.

"My charge is elsewhere. And I will fulfill it now, now that I see hope in you. You, and your new friends, can turn the tides on Apollyon. Will you do this for me, Jude, Prophet?"

Jude gripped his notebook tighter in his fingers and nodded his head with a smile. Aquarius smiled back down at him.

"One more thing I should tell you," Aquarius looked around as though he didn't want anyone to hear, prompting Jude to lean in closer as though the two were sharing a secret.

"My return will be...a sore spot for my brothers and sisters. I would ask that you keep this meeting of ours between you and I, until I make myself known to them again." Aquarius suddenly looked more serious, his features seems to change slightly, and even his hair appeared to darken just a few shades.

"Can I trust you with this?"

Jude nodded slowly, lowering his own eyebrows in attempt to make his face appear more serious as well.

"Absolutely. I won't tell a soul." He said, even lowering his voice a bit.

"Fantastic. You are everything a steward should be," Aquarius straightened up again. "I have nothing but admiration for you humans. And I have the utmost faith in your ability, Jude. I must bid you farewell for now, but I trust we will see each other again soon."

Aquarius bowed low again, and Jude stood awkwardly, unsure if he should bow too or not. Then in an instant, Aquarius was gone, and Jude was alone again among the giant trees.

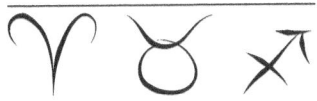

Aries peered into the forest in the direction Jude had gone and cocked her head almost unnoticeably. She could not see Jude through the trees, which in and of itself was strange, since material objects never blocked her sight. But more than that, Aries sensed that Jude was not alone in the forest; there was most definitely another presence among the trees with the Prophet.

She listened beyond the back and forth of Riku and Samantha, who were discussing their next moves both as a team and individually. There were birds chirping and a snake several meters off and wind blowing, and somewhere fifty meters or so away a blank emptiness, void of sound and life.

Someone was masking their presence in a way that directly blocked Aries' senses. There were only two beings in creation that could do such a thing, one being another Zodiac, and the other Apollyon. There would be no need for another Zodiac to hide their presence, but it was possible Apollyon had found them and had come to finish what he started in San Francisco.

"I shall return in a moment," Aries said to her two companions, who both looked at her and nodded without need for another word or explantation. She strode with great purpose from the small clearing, her hand crossing her waist to grip the handle of her dagger. But she didn't get far before Jude appeared from around one of the trees.

"Whoa, hey now. Just me. Prophet." Jude waved, seeing the intense look in the Zodiac's eyes.

"Who was with you?" Aries demanded.

"With me? No one."

"I sensed the presence of another. Was it the Destroyer?"

"The guy that smashed my face into the street? Oh yeah, he popped in to apologize. Then we got to talking about raid dungeons in this new MMO..." Jude trailed off.

"Apollyon would not apologize," Aries said sternly. Jude lowered his eyebrows as he tried to decide whether or not she was joking.

"Aries...it was a joke. No, Apollyon was not with me in the forest."

"Then who?"

"No one. A couple of birds. I saw a squirrel." Jude fought back the sudden urge to swallow hard, thinking that might be a dead giveaway. Aries peered at him and then behind him, slowly removing her hand from her dagger.

"Were you writing in your Tome?" Her voice softened a bit.

"Uh...yeah, I was actually. Just hoped no one would follow me. Or bother me. That kind of thing."

"Then I am satisfied."

"You are?"

"Yes. I could neither see nor hear you in the forest. As though someone was blocking you from my senses. Your abilities are quite refined, Prophet." Aries smiled down at him.

"Yeah, so I've been told," Jude swallowed and cleared his throat. "So," he said as he stepped past Aries and back into the clearing with the others. "Anyone have a game plan? My last one, didn't work so well."

"Not true!" Riku exclaimed. "Your fault only was in your lack of trust in your partners. We are a team! We must come together to fight as one."

Samantha sighed.

"You know, he's right. And that little angel stunt thing you did actually helped. But next time, *tell* me what you're doing." Samantha crossed her arms over her chest, and gave Jude a look.

"Okay, yes, you're both right. So then, what's next?"

"I need a few more answers about…me," Samantha started. "The lady in Egypt that gave me this," she pointed to the armband, "knew a lot about the Zodiac. They have records from the last Prophet detailing a few things."

Jude perked up at hearing this.

"Seriously? Like what kind of stuff?"

"I don't know. I wasn't really paying attention last time to be honest. This was all kind of sudden. But I'll find out what I can."

"And I go to train," Riku smiled, puffing his chest out as much as he could. "I know the fight will come again soon, and I will be ready to do my best alongside my friends."

There is no breaking this guy, is there? Jude thought.

"Good. You saved my butt in Wyoming. We might need more of that. I've got some things to go over with Taurus, maybe do a little more past-surfing. Or whatever it is he does to me." Taurus nodded his head once at Jude, and almost made what looked like a smile.

"Great, so let's keep in touch or something. You guys can do that, right?" Samantha gestured to the Zodiac.

"We sense one another's presence, yes," Sagittarius answered. "But on this planet our connection is somewhat limited."

"Done. I have just added you both as friends on my phone," Riku beamed at the others and showed them his phone. "Text me when you need saving."

Jude looked down at his mobile phone and smirked.

"Wow, okay then. We're connected too."

"Great, then let's meet up in a few hours or so. Sound good?" Samantha patted Riku on the shoulder, eliciting a red glow from his face.

"Sensei, I'm ready to go now," Riku quickly and awkwardly made for Sagittarius' side. The Archer drew his bow and loosed a glowing arrow. Riku gave one last glance to Samantha before he vanished from sight.

"I guess we're next. Aries, do the honors?" Samantha took hold of Aries' arm and they vanished from sight as well.

"Was there something specific you needed to see, Prophet?" Taurus asked.

"Yeah actually. Oh, but hang on one second." Jude opened his notebook and began scribbling furiously, intent and focused on every word that went down on the page. Once he was finished he inspected his work and, feeling satisfied, slammed the notebook shut.

"There," he said, "now I'm ready."

"What would you like to see?"

"You know, I really want to go back to Atlantis."

"Atlantis? But you've already seen its fate." Taurus cocked head, a little confused.

"Yes but, there's something else I need to see. Maybe a few days before everything fell apart?"

Taurus placed his hand on Jude's shoulder and nodded.

"Then back to Atlantis we shall go."

Jude smiled and, as he gave one last look over his shoulder to the empty forest, felt someone watching him in the distance. He nodded and looked back up to Taurus.

"Ready when you are."

And then the forest was empty once more.

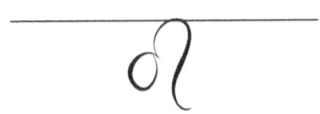

Calleigh Morrison never did like warmer weather, so when a post in Hammerfest, Norway came available at her archaeological research company, she jumped at the chance. Originally born in Scotland, Calleigh spent more time digging through the dirt than playing with dolls or wearing dresses. Though much to the dismay of her mother, her father encouraged her rough behavior.

Her mother was pleased when she announced her acceptance to the University of Glasgow, but disappointed that she'd be studying with the Strathearn Environs and Royal Forteviot, or SERF, project in Field Archaeology. She had struggled to make a name for herself amidst the male dominated career she had chosen, and almost gave up a few times a

long the way. But now, as she was about to turn forty years old, Calleigh was one of the top archaeologists in the UK.

She checked and double checked her gear as she waited for the boat that would ferry her and her team to the remote island Bjørnøya, three hundred kilometers north of their base camp. The tiny island, only sixteen kilometers long, was recently discovered to be a temporary settlement for Vikings centuries ago. Given the latest news of disaster coming out of France, Calleigh was eager to make some new, more positive, headlines.

As she went over her gear and scanned down a list on her tablet, she heard the heavy thudding of footsteps drawing nearer to her. She kept working and didn't say a word until the steps stopped right next to her side.

"If ya aren't ready to go, George, by th' time our ferry gets 'ere I'm gonna pop ya upside the skull like I did las' night." She said in her thick Scottish accent.

"Calleigh," came a deep voice she didn't quite recognize, "the time has come to join destiny."

"Oh aye? Well then destiny better have its bags packed too, or I swear to the Virgin Mother you'll be swimmin' to Bjørnøya in your skivvies." Calleigh finally turned her eyes from her tablet and came face to face with the chest of Leo. "Oh!"

"I've been searching for you, Calleigh. I am Leo, the Lion, one of the twelve Timeless Zodiac. And you are The Purifier." Leo smiled down at her through his thick blonde beard.

Calleigh looked awkwardly around him to see if anyone else was nearby before she gave a nervous chuckle and cleared her throat.

"Leo…the Lion, ya say? Well you're a tall drink of somethin', but I dunno about a lion now. Did Charlie put ya up to this? If he did, you can go right back an' tell him I dinna mean what I said about his drunken proposal last week."

"His proposal?" Leo smirked.

"Aye, about gettin' married to a giant before I'd marry 'im." Calleigh turned her head, but then stole another glance at the larger than life man that stood before her. "Not that ya aren't impressive…just Charlie is a small man, an' I like more meat on my men. So you go right back an' tell him the answer is still 'no'".

Leo smiled even brighter and chuckled a little, inspired by her attitude.

"Every age the people of this Earth amaze me. There have been billions of you, and yet you're each so unique in your own way." He shook his head and rested both hands on his hips.

"I do wish we had more time, though. Unfortunately, that is not the case. Your skills and understanding are needed elsewhere."

"Now yer jus' tryin' to flatter me," she swallowed hard as her cheeks turned rosy pink. Her accent was even thicker as she fought to contain the girly demeanor that came out now and again from under her rough visage.

"But you do have skills," Leo went on. "You have the ability to see what is buried and bring to life what was lost. You can take what was broken and make it new again. My task is to fan the flame of your talents, to sharpen them, and make them more than they ever were."

"Ah," Calleigh stood motionless, staring in disbelief at the large man mountain before her. "Aye, ya aren't too heart broken then, when I tell ya yer full of it."

"But it's the truth, Calleigh Morrison. I will unlock the power hidden within…"

"See, there ya lost me," she interrupted. "I almost woulda' listened, but ya blew it when ya mentioned the 'power within'. I know a pervert when I see one."

Leo was visibly taken aback. That Scottish charm also had a bite to it, so it seemed. Nevertheless, there was an urgency building up inside Leo that he hadn't experienced before. Every age, he carried out his charge to the utmost of his abilities. Even enduring one failure after another, and being forced to watch civilization after civilization crumble and fall at the hands of the Darkness, he never wavered. But neither did he ever feel the strange sense that filled him now.

His encounter with Aquarius after centuries of silence from his brother had shaken him a little, but it wasn't that which now plagued that back of his mind. Something else was pushing him to snatch up this little human and run...South.

"What proof," Leo started after regaining his composure and clearing his throat, "would you like me to offer to prove my sincerity?"

Calleigh raised an eyebrow then rolled her eyes.

"Still lookin' to go after that power hidden within, eh? Fine. But I don't think ya can get back that credibility with me, not even if the Pope himself was standing 'ere, vouching for ya."

"Hmmmm." Leo smirked.

In an instant and with a flutter of snow from the ground he vanished and reappeared, and along with him the Pope of the Roman Catholic Church.

"Holy Mother! It's the Holy Father!" Calleigh shouted as she quickly crossed herself and panicked. "Uh, forgive the outburst, your Worship, I dinna expect ya would really pop in like that!"

Leo crossed his arms and nodded his head at his accomplishment.

"Now do you believe me?"

"Escusi," the Pope started, as he looked around clearly confused and quite alarmed.

"Ah yes," Leo touched the startled Pope on the shoulder and he was gone. He turned his attention back to Calleigh, whose pale skin had turned several shades of red.

"I dunno who or what ya are, but I dinna sign up for this." Calleigh said as she began to back away.

"Allow me to be clear, then." Leo stooped down lower, coming eye to eye with Calleigh. "The world is in peril. You can help. Will you?"

Calleigh stared back into the large face of the Zodiac. None of this made any kind of sense, but there was a truthfulness in his big eyes. She had been watching on the news the reports about an event taking place in Paris, where the city was under some kind of attack. And then hours ago similar reports were coming from the United States about the city of San Francisco. If any of this, or all of it, was connected with this man-mountain, perhaps he was telling the truth, and there was something she could do about something.

She closed her eyes and let out a big sigh, then opened one eye to check if Leo was still there. He was.

"All right. I dunno what ya think I can do, but I'm willin' to find out." She raised her hands up to her sides. "So what do we do now?"

Leo offered his hand. Reluctantly, Calleigh put her small right hand into Leo's large one. He smiled broadly under his big blonde beard, and with a puff of snow around them, they vanished.

Chapter 4

Samantha opened her eyes after feeling her insides turned inside out, a somewhat familiar feeling she attributed to "teleporting" with Aries across large spaces. The two were back in front of the Grand Egyptian Museum, in Cairo. There weren't many people outside the great building, so no one seemed to notice Samantha pop into existence out of thin air. And of course no one but herself was able to see the armor-clad giant of a woman that was Aries standing next to her.

They made their way into the the front doors only to be stopped by a middle-aged Egyptian man who spoke very poor English. He tried to stop them from walking past the security gates muttering something that sounded like "closing", but Samantha just kept repeating herself in a louder, New Yorker tone.

"I can't hear you! Doctor Saliba! I'm looking for Doctor Saliba! Do you know *her*? Can you get *her*? Doctor Saliba!"

Finally the man gave in and stepped away while speaking furiously into his walkie talkie and held a palm up to Samantha.

"You changed your accent," Aries commented.

"I'm from Ohio, but a few years driving an ambulance in Brooklyn teaches you a few things," Samantha whispered just loud enough so she knew Aries could hear. The man turned his palm and waved her through, without so much as looking her in the face.

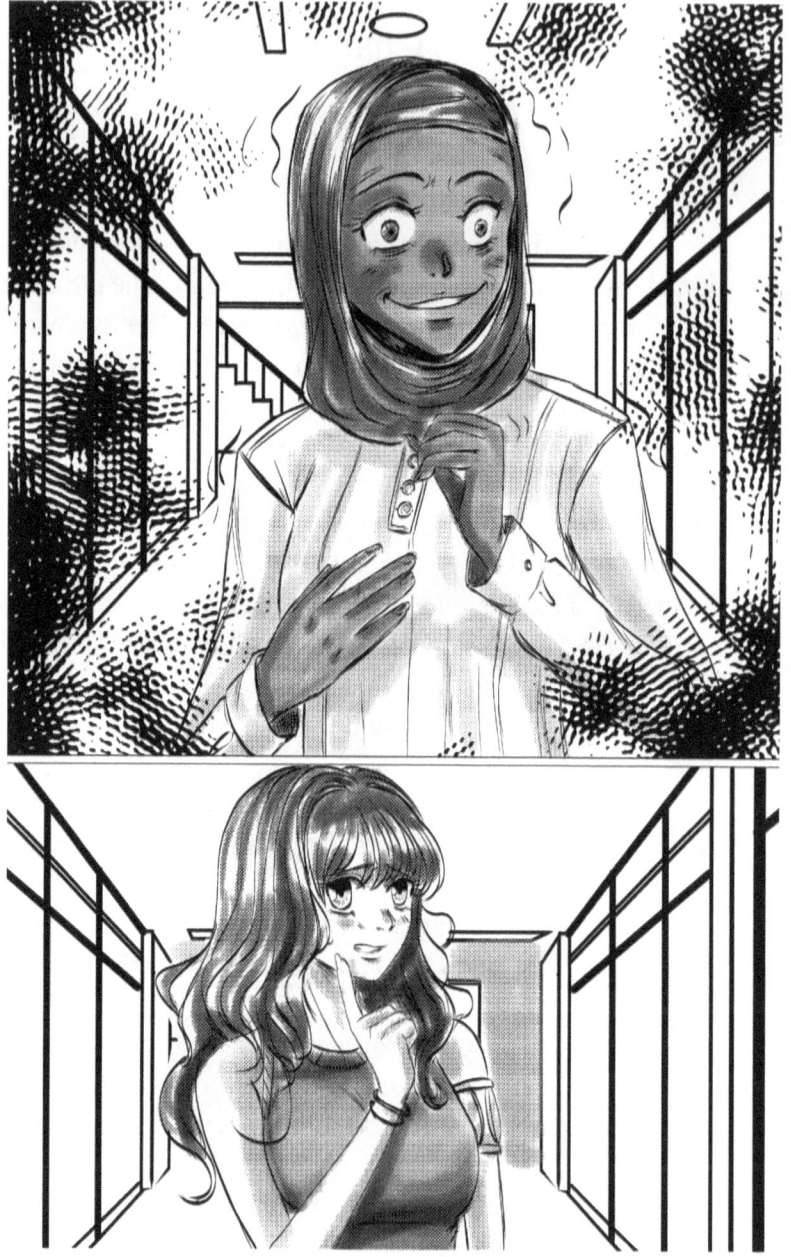

"Thank you!" Samantha said, leaning close to the man and patting him on the shoulder. He glared at her and scowled as she walked by. "I sure hope this lady has some more information. Otherwise this trip was a waste, 'cause I think that guy just gave me the curse of the mummy."

"I can counter any curses placed upon you," Aries answered, in her normal straight laced style.

"Oh. That's…good." Samantha was relieved to see the smiling face of Dr. Saliba waiting for them at the end of the long walkway.

"Doctor, I know this must be unusual, but thank you for seeing me." Samantha shook the woman's hand, finding it a little cold.

"My pleasure," Dr. Saliba smiled at Samantha, taking no notice of Aries. "I'm very happy to see you. How can I help?"

"You mentioned before that there are records? From the other prophet that came before ours?"

"The other prophet…" Dr. Saliba stared at Samantha oddly.

"We were downstairs…" Samantha made a face, also trying to remember exactly where they went within the massive complex.

"Oh yes," Dr. Saliba said with a nod. "The storage room. Silly me. How could I forget?" She smiled, and turned to guide the two towards the elevators. "That's a beautiful armband you're wearing," Dr. Saliba said causally. "We have many similar artifacts here in the museum…" she trailed off as they approached the elevators.

Samantha stopped cold, prompting Aries to do the same.

"Does she seem, off, to you?" Samantha whispered to Aries.

"Strictly speaking, all humans seem a bit off to us." Aries said. Samantha sighed and continued on as they entered the elevator.

As before, Aries waited outside the elevator as the door closed with only the two women inside. There was a stunned silence as they rode down into the basement levels of the museum. Samantha couldn't place exactly what was wrong, but she knew Dr. Saliba was acting strangely.

The elevator came to a stop and the doors opened, with Aries waiting for the two. Dr. Saliba walked out of the elevator without so much as a glance in Aries' direction, a stark contrast to their first meeting where she was both shocked and delighted to see the Zodiac waiting for them in the basement. Samantha followed, but at a distance, as they worked their way down the many twisting halls of the lower levels.

As they finally came to a stop at the dead end, Samantha recognized from before, Dr. Saliba merely stood there, motionless, staring at the wall.

"Um, are you okay, doctor?" Samantha asked gently, leaning a bit closer.

Dr. Saliba spun on her heels and smiled wide eyed at her, with an expression that insinuated insanity.

"Silly me. I forgot how to get in for a moment," she said, spinning back and lowering her face to the pyramid shaped design on the door. A few beeps later, and the secret door opened with a hiss.

"Please, after you," she said to Samantha, as she bowed low and stepped out of the way.

"Sure. Right." Samantha sidestepped past the bowing doctor and entered into the vault. It was just as before, although some of the containers and crates were sitting wide open, as though someone was going through them looking for something.

"So, which one is it?" Samantha stopped and turned to find Dr. Saliba directly behind her.

"Which one? Which one? Which…one." Dr. Saliba grinned, her face suddenly more dark that before. "The words of The Prophet were painted on the tablet, not chiseled. He was dying, you see." She began to walk slowly closer to Samantha, who started backpedaling.

"Okay you're really starting to freak me right the hell out…"

"He lost his chisel. So he touched his forehead with these two fingers," Dr. Saliba held up her pointer and middle finger. "He dabbed the blood from his head, and wrote on the tablets."

Suddenly Samantha remembered Dr. Saliba telling her that the records of The Prophet were poorly preserved. It made sense now, if the records were written not in stone but on it, and with blood, that over time the words would fade. As she continued to back away from the encroaching doctor she looked over to Aries, who stood motionless, watching.

"Hey, Aries, maybe we should just go, hmm?" But Aries did not answer. She watched the two women with the utmost concentration, but made no effort to budge from where she stood.

"Blood fades. Washes away. Time. Dirt. *Ssssand.*" Dr. Saliba hissed. A hiss all too familiar to Samantha. Now it made sense why Aries stood still, and why the doctor was act-ing so strange. She wasn't the doctor at all.

"Rezzek," Samantha almost spit the name out as she said it. Dr. Saliba's grin widened to an inhuman degree. Her eyes started to bulge as though they might at any moment pop right out of their sockets. She opened her mouth wide, wider than any human ought to be able to do, and a swarm of flies burst out from deep in her throat.

Samantha jumped back immediately, pushed a nearby table between the two and crouched low as the swarm of flies grew larger. Within a few mere moments they had stopped altogether, and Dr. Saliba slumped to the floor, whether unconscious or dead, Samantha wasn't sure.

The flies spun in a torrent and gathered together until they took on the form of a man, coat, hat and all. The Hatman, Rezzek, as Samantha had come to know him, now stood a few meters away. His gaunt face, and empty, dark eyes, facing the floor. His evil, toothy, wide smile almost painted on.

"*So good to sssee you my dear. Yes, so good indeed.*" Rezzek hissed.

"I've been called a few things," Samantha began, "but don't you ever call me your 'dear'".

"*Oh, sweet Healer. I was not talking to you.*" Rezzek said, as he turned his gaze to Aries. "*No response? No pithy comeback? Why, you look downright frozen,*" Rezzek chuckled an eerie laugh that made Samantha's skin crawl.

"*She told you, did she not? They are unable, forbidden even, from interfering directly with the Master's planssss. She will have to just stand there, helpless, and watch you die!*"

Samantha didn't stick around to hear the rest, but bolted down a long line of tables for the elevator. She reached it quickly, with no attempt to stop her from Rezzek, which immediately worried her as she tapped the call button on the wall. But the doors did not open, and the elevator made no sounds of coming at all.

Samantha turned her back to the door and watched as Rezzek stood before Aries, even with his larger than normal stature still looked up at the Zodiac. He was whispering something, admiring her, and gave little attention to Samantha.

You bastard, she thought. *Biding your time, huh?*

Samantha gently pushed off from the elevator doors, the only motion that could have made her move towards the Hatman, and started back across the floor.

"Hey, prune face!" She yelled. Rezzek didn't pay her any mind. "Did your *master* tell you how I threw him into a building? Apollyon, that's his name right?"

At mention of Apollyon, Rezzek sharply turned his head towards Samantha.

"Yeah, that was it. Must have been embarrassing for him. Little old girl like me, human girl, tossing your *master* away like a piece of trash."

Rezzek hissed loud like a threatened snake. He turned away form Aries completely and started towards Samantha.

"Human filth!" he spat. *"You are not worthy to sssspeak the name of the Master!"*

"Worthy or not, I can say his name all day long if I want. I just don't want to. It's not *worth* the effort to say the name of a pansy that gets thrown around by a girl like me."

The lights in the room began to flicker, as a strange black smoke began to appear in the air from everywhere. Samantha glanced at Aries, who very, very slowly turned her head towards the two of them as the space between them lessened.

"I was told to come here. To wait for you. To kill you. But I sssseee now that you do not deserve something as final, as fitting, as sssssweet as death." Rezzek hissed as he waved

one hand, causing one of the tables in his way to slide several meters across the floor.

"Not that you could kill me if you wanted to," Samantha taunted, though she stopped in her tracks and decided to hold her position for now.

"*Ha,*" Rezzek continued forward. "*No no, instead I think I'll crawl inside you. Through your nose, your ears, your mouth, and tear your soul apart piece by piece from the inside.*"

"Crawl inside me? Hey now, you haven't even bought me dinner. What kind of pervert are you anyway?" Samantha watched in the corner of her eye as Aries' eyes began to glow, to burn, as she was now fixed on Rezzek.

"*You will scream. You will cry. You will beg for death. And I will give you only more pain. More ssssuffering. More agony!*" Rezzek sounded somewhat delighted as he waved his hand again, and the final table that stood between the two of them slid to the side.

"About that," Samantha took a step back. "Is that the will of your *master,* or is that yours?"

Rezzek stopped. His smile disappeared. He swiveled his head to his right side and in an instant Aries was on him.

"Vile worm!" She cried, grabbing him by the throat and lifting him off the ground. "I cannot kill you," she said, drawing her dagger, "but you are correct. There *are* things worse than death!"

The dagger burst into flame, and she thrust it into Rezzek's torso. He screamed a scream that was deafening to Samantha. She covered her ears but the scream seemed to penetrate her mind as well.

The Hatman, coat, hat and all, burst into red and white flames that swirled around him like a tornado. The roaring of the fire drowned out the sound of his cries, and Samantha rose to her feet to watch him writhe and squirm in Aries' firm grip.

"What you were, what *we* were, is no more! So I will burn what heart is left in you again and again! Tell your master to send someone *worthy* next time! You rotting piece of..."

Rezzek exploded into a million flies, each of them on fire, as they frantically buzzed and swarmed in attempt to flee. The next moment, they found the air duct and stormed it so fiercely that the grate covering fell to the floor. And then they were gone.

Samantha was still trembling twenty minutes after the whole ordeal, so she had tried to calm her nerves by tending to the various boxes, cabinets, and crates that had been opened. Whatever it was Rezzek was looking for, he hadn't found it. That thought gave Samantha hope, but also made her unnerved that neither would she be able to locate the tablets without the help of the curator.

Unfortunately, the curator, Dr. Saliba, was indeed dead. When the flies had finally left the room Samantha had darted to where the doctor lay on the floor. No pulse, no breathing, and her low body temperature all told Samantha that she had been dead for some time now. That explained why their handshake was so cold, but didn't explain how the woman was able to walk, speak, blink, breathe...all the normal things a person very much alive would be doing.

"He is not human, not anymore," Aries said, as though reading Samantha's mind as she searched the cabinets, and her brain, for answers. "Rezzek was able to possess the body of Dr. Saliba. It is very likely he also was the one to kill her."

"Possess? Like, demon or ghost or something?" Samantha turned to face Aries and crossed her arms, hoping for answers from somewhere.

"Rezzek has been granted powers from unnatural forces."

"Yeah, you don't say. How about you spill a little more. Because this crap is getting old. Just who is that guy?"

"His name is Rezzek," Aries began.

"I caught that part. Why is he trying to kill me? How does he know you? Look I get it. If I had an ex-boyfriend like that, I wouldn't bring him up either. But this is twice now."

Much to Samantha's surprise, so much so she couldn't say another word, Aries sat down. Given her height she sat on one of the display cases that came up to Samantha at the waist, but it was still a shock nonetheless. Aries stared at the floor for a time before she finally spoke again.

"You live such fragile lives," Aries said. "In a few short years you are born, you live, you die, and are forgotten by all who knew you." Aries forced a smile and looked over at Samantha, whose mouth was hanging open. Aries batted her eyes and turned her face back towards the floor.

"Yet in that fragile, tiny space of time, you are all so beautiful. We Timeless Zodiac have existed since before the earth was made, and we will continue long after it is unmade. I have witnessed billions of human lives, and you are all so unique. I am unchanging, but you can be whatever you chose."

Samantha felt a tugging inside her that almost literally pulled her to the floor. She sat, cross-legged, with her eyes never leaving her teacher.

"Okay, go on," Samantha urged.

"Rezzek was a man, once. His ancestors were no-madic, traveling across frozen plains and even a frozen ocean before settling in what is now your country. He was born with a touch of destiny upon him, he was to be The Guardian. But when Apollyon came to tear apart that civilization and bring the Darkness, he lured Rezzek with promises of power. And Rezzek was lost."

Aries stared off a few moments as though remembering something deeply painful.

"So if he was the Guardian, who trained him?" Samantha asked.

"I did," Aries answered right away. Samantha stood up.

"Wait, but you train The Healer, right?"

"Every age is different. We find our steward and carry out our charge, but we do not decide the fate for each." Aries said.

"So you trained him, and he…went to the…dark side, I guess? But the way he kept talking, like you two were, a little more than, teacher and student."

"We Zodiac are not without emotions. If that were so, you humans would be nothing more than a task to complete, and battling the Chaos would be nothing more than a game. We win, we lose, it never matters, because it would be a game." Aries stood again and turned to face Samantha.

"But we *can* feel. We *can* hurt. And we *can* love. I loved Rezzek, and he me, for his part. So his betrayal stings all the more, and Apollyon knows this. Rezzek betrayed his brethren, and they were forced to strike him down, and forced to kill the great tree Yggdrasil. But when they killed him, they only struck an empty shell. His soul already belonged to Apollyon."

"Is that why you can't really kill him?" Samantha asked.

"Partly, yes. We are forbidden from directly interfering with Apollyon's plans. Only you stewards can do so." Aries smiled down at Samantha as she got closer.

"Does that mean…one of us can actually kill him? For good?" Samantha craned her neck to look up at the Zodiac as Aries beamed down upon her.

"Rezzek's soul belongs to the Chaotic One, now. He will do with it as he pleases." Aries looked away. "And torment me in the process."

Samantha grabbed Aries by the arms, as high up as she could reach, and tried to turn the Zodiac to look at her. She suddenly felt how strong and powerful Aries was, and couldn't imagine there would be much this giant being could not do.

"I've watched you burn him alive, twice. I've heard him scream so loud it hurt my brain. Whatever he was to you, he's not that anymore. But if you can't kill him, and I can, I will."

Aries smiled down at Samantha, her eyes seemed to say everything was going to be alright, child.

"Everything is going to be alright, child," Aries said. "You are The Healer. Your focus should be on healing those that are afflicted because of the Darkness."

Samantha felt at peace, and she slowly let go of Aries. She looked around at the somewhat fixed mess in the room and shrugged.

"Well I guess I've done all I could here. We better go before someone finds Dr. Saliba…and me. There's already surveillance I'm sure with my big face on it." Samantha took one last look around. "It's a shame we didn't find those tablets though. I really did want to…"

Aries held out a hand and the floor a few meters away began to shake lightly. A false floor suddenly flew away and crashed into one of the cabinets and a hidden safe began to rise on a lift. Samantha watched in surprise and shock as the lift raised until the full safe, about two meters in height, was revealed. Aries drew her dagger and cut the hinges off the solid metal door like a hot knife slicing through butter.

Samantha took hold of the handle, and with a tug the door came loose and crashed, rather loudly, to the floor. Inside were four separate shelves, each with a purple velvet bag. Samantha grabbed one and pulled it out, nearly dropping it.

"Holy crap, what are these made of?" She said as she opened the bag.

"Gold," Aries said, just as the bag was opened. Inside were three tablets made of solid gold, roughly forty centimeters long, twenty wide and seven centimeters thick. There was writing on each tablet in a language Samantha couldn't even begin to understand, in a dark red color.

"Is that, blood?" she asked.

"Yes it is. The last Prophet wrote in blood because he, as Rezzek said, was dying. He used gold for all his tomes, because gold does not rust. And he knew whomever found them after he was long gone would not endeavor to quickly destroy them."

"This is amazing. Each one of these bags?"

"All four bags, yes". Aries said, as she pulled out the others and set them on the ground before Samantha.

"There's no way I can carry all these."

"Of course there is. You will have help," Aries smiled at her, then she picked up all four bags as easily as though they were feathers.

"Good. Now let's get out of here." Samantha said, taking Aries' arm.

Chapter 5

Calleigh's scream could be heard for a solid kilometer as she and Leo appeared on Ross Island in Antarctica. She spun around and turned her head frantically left and right as she tried to discern just where they now were. The two stood on a sheet of ice and snow, and there was ice every direction she looked, with the only change in scenery being that of the island itself as it rose up out of the ocean, and the only wildlife were hundreds of startled penguins.

"Where the bloody hell are we?!" she shouted at Leo as she gave him a hard shove. He didn't budge, but let out a laugh instead.

"Antarctica. I thought you enjoyed the snow!" he chuckled.

"No. No this inn't possible. We were in Hammerfest jus' a moment ago. Did ya slip me somethin' in my coffee? You drugged me, dinna ya?" Calleigh backed away from Leo, pointing her finger at him.

"I brought you the Pope. Wasn't that enough to prove my intentions? You said you were willing to see what you could do. This is where you find that out." Leo smiled broadly.

Calleigh slowly lowered her hand and gave the place a few more looks. She shook her head in disbelief and pointed at a penguin that was watching her intently. She let out a heavy sigh and turned back to Leo.

"Alright then, can ya at least tell me where we are?"

"We are standing on an ice sheet, over the ocean. Twenty-five kilometers from the McMurdo Station. That little mountain there," Leo pointed to the peaks nearby, "is Ross Island. That's where you and I are headed."

"We're standin' on the ocean? Right now?" Calleigh asked.

"Yes. Yes we are."

"I guess that's one off the bucket list. Ha. Never thought I'd be walkin' on water. And we're goin' there?" She pointed to the island.

"Right there, actually," Leo said, pointing to a lower peak. "It's not that far, only thirty-four kilometers."

"Oh aye, *only*. And ya expect me to run all the way?" Calleigh gave him a look.

"Of course not. You can walk instead."

Calleigh rolled her eyes and pointed at the peak.

"So what's up there that's so important?"

"That place is known as Mount Terror…"

"Mount what now?!" Calleigh screamed, backing away again.

"Mount Terror. It's an old volcano…oh don't make that face. The volcano has been dormant for ages. But it's through there that you'll find the path you've been meant for." Leo smiled as he looked up at the small peak.

"Okay. So let's say I do believe you. Ya did bring me the Pope, I 'spose. And let's say I believe this inn't some dream I'm in. What *exactly* am I going to find up on…Mount Terror?"

Leo's smile faded. He blinked and looked down at the snow a moment, furrowed his eyebrows and turned to face Calleigh. His expression did not give her a great sense of security.

Page 48

"I…I am not sure." Leo finally said.

"Ya aren't sure!? Ya dragged me all the way to the other side of the world, I was supposed to be on the *North* pole by now, by the way, and ya want me to climb a volcano called 'Mount Terror', but ya don't even know why?!" With every other word, Calleigh gave Leo a shove to the chest. Not that it did anything to budge him, but she was starting to enjoy putting her hands on his massive frame.

Leo growled low in his throat, a deep guttural growl that showed his annoyance in his own ability to remember as he ignored Calleigh but stared intently at Mount Terror. But the growl was loud enough, and not entirely unlike a lion, that Calleigh paused in her shove attacks and pulled her hands back very slowly, just in case his annoyance turned towards her.

"Why…why can I not remember what lies there?" Leo said, more to himself than to Calleigh. "I see all things I need to see. Your path as The Purifier is clear to me, but why here? Why this place?"

"Ya dinna tell me. I dunno what 'The Purifier' means anyhow." Calleigh said as she reached out and gently patted Leo on the chest, just to reassure him.

"Cistern…" He said, staring off across the ice and snow as the wind began to pick up. "Cistern. Aquarius. The Cistern!" Leo bellowed. He grabbed Calleigh suddenly and flung her over to his back. She yelped and wrapped her arms around his neck and clung on in a piggy-back fashion. She was immediately thankful Leo couldn't see her face, as she was certain it was several of shades blush, and not from the cold.

"There isn't time for you to walk, after all, Purifier. Come, ride me and I'll explain on the way!" With that, Leo took off running across the frozen sheet.

"Oh…aye. Sure I'll just…ride then." Even saying the words made Calleigh flush even more.

Leo covered amazing amounts of ground as he strode effortlessly across ice and snow. Calleigh buried most her face in the fur lining of his vest that covered his shoulders to avoid the cold wind. But even as they ran, Leo spoke loud enough that Calleigh had no trouble hearing his words, even with the icy gusts.

"We Zodiac have bestowed gifts to the stewards over the ages," he began. "Each relic became a tool for future stewards, and a right of passage as it were."

"You said the word 'cistern'. What's that?" Calleigh screamed over Leo's shoulder to fight the noise of the wind.

"The Zodiac Aquarius, the Water Bearer, created the Cistern as a means to focus the abilities of The Purifier. But it's been lost to us for ages."

"Lost how?"

"I do not remember. And that troubles me. Aquarius paid me a visit as I hunted for you…"

"Wait what?! You were hunting me?!"

Leo let out a loud laugh that seemed to echo off the island before them and carry over the icy plain.

"I am Leo, the Lion, am I not?" He slowed his great strides a bit as they got closer to the island. "I had not seen my brother Aquarius for many ages. But his sudden appearance was made more mysterious when he confessed to have hidden the Cistern away."

Calleigh shook her head. None of this really made much sense to her. But the evidence was piling up that

Page 50

something beyond her current understanding was happening. She knew that Paris had been attacked by some outside force not yet explained. She knew that San Francisco had also recently been attacked, and was still in a state of lockdown by the United States military.

There were forces at work that she didn't comprehend, but if not for those other news headlines, and even with the sudden appearance of the Pope, she never would have trusted this giant of a man with her life. Even if he was somewhat enticing...

"So if Aquarius made the Cistern for...me, I 'spose, why would he hide it?"

"I do not know. But he insisted I find it."

"Did he tell you where to find it?"

"No."

"Then why the bloody hell are we in Antarctica in the first place?!" Leo chuckled again at Calleigh's spirit.

"Something drew me here. I cannot explain that either, which troubles me even more. But you have purpose here and I'll see that you discover that purpose."

Leo stopped cold, and looked up at the peak. He nodded in approval of his own efforts, and gave a quick look back to where they can come. His great footsteps were already being covered over with snow carried on the wind.

"You can hike from here, I think," Leo said as he reached back and plucked Calleigh by her jacket, swung her over his back and planted her on her feet with a thud. "The dormant volcano is just ahead. Yes. That is where we'll find it."

"Find what exactly?"

"The door," Leo said flatly as he began to hike. Confused even more than before, Calleigh started after him.

"What door? Ya said you dinna know what was 'ere! That's a volcano ya know."

"Save your breath, Purifier. We still have eighteen kilometers to go."

"*What?!*"

Riku watched a somewhat familiar landscape zoom into view, and moments later he found himself standing on firm ground in a large field with mountains in the distance. He was home.

Standing next to him, atop his black steed, was the Zodiac Sagittarius, dressed in full samurai regalia as always. Riku smiled and closed his eyes, breathed a deep breath of the humid air and fell backwards onto the grass. For the first time in his memory, Riku was pleased to be home in Japan.

"Catch your breath," said Sagittarius, breaking the calm moment. "You have much work to do."

"What work?" Riku craned his neck to look at the archer upside-down.

"You must train."

"I've spent my whole life training. Let me rest or give me a fight."

"You've trained against dummies. You've trained against single opponents." Sagittarius nocked an arrow from thin air on his bow and loosed it into the grass a few meters away. "But you must become faster, stronger." Another arrow several meters from that one.

"Do you know the next target?" Riku rolled onto his stomach and watched two more arrows find their place.

"I do not. The Prophet will know, however. You must be ready when he contacts you."

Riku scoffed and got off his belly, brushed himself off and found himself standing in the exact middle of a circle of half a dozen arrows sticking out of the ground.

"Jude's plan didn't work last time. Why should I trust it to work now?"

"His plan was faulty, but his intelligence was accurate. He knew where and when the enemy would strike," Sagittarius said as he exited the circle. "Now, prepare yourself!"

Riku lazily drew his sword and took his stance. The wind picked up suddenly as Sagittarius swung his bow twice over his head in wide circles before slashing it down to one side. The arrows began to glow.

"What is…"

Before Riku could finish his sentence, each arrow, starting with the first and working in a circle around him, sprung to life, grew, and took the shape of a warrior. Each glowed a different and distinct color; one topaz, one amethyst, one ruby, one sapphire, one turquoise, and the final, a silvery tin color.

"These are your sparring companions," said Sagittarius proudly. Each image drew a sword, all identical to the one Riku held. "Each was once The Warrior, like yourself. Each wielded the Sword of Achilles, like yourself. But unlike them, you will succeed in stopping the Chaos."

"None of these guys beat Apollyon?" Riku asked. If the mask had been removed, Riku was certain Sagittarius would be frowning right now.

"No. They all had…successes in their time. But none have ever stopped the Darkness from spreading. So you must!"

Each image took a different stance, though all looked ready for a fight. Riku took his traditional kendo stance and tried to see his opponents behind him, but his rigid legs and shoulders made that impossible.

"You face the fiercest Warriors this world has known. Many you may know, but most have been forgotten in time." Sagittarius pointed to a large man, glowing red, wearing a toga, tightly wrapped around his legs, groin and chest. "Heracles."

"What? Hercules?!" Riku burst out, now more fan-boy than Warrior.

"Achilles." Sagittarius pointed to a man clad in thin, Roman-looking leather armor, glowing amethyst.

"Li Hou," he announced pointing his bow at a the tin-colored figure who resembled a Chinese farmer in simple clothing.

Riku faced the tin man and bowed.

"M'laku." Riku turned to face a very thin, tall, African man who glowed topaz and wore only a loin cloth.

"Gideon," Sagittarius announced the turquoise image of a man wearing a tunic, belt and sandals. "And finally Yngvild."

Riku faced the final image, colored Sapphire, and stopped cold.

"A woman?" Riku looked the image up and down carefully. She wore cloth pants, a tunic tied with a leather belt, and various pieces of armor, leather as far as Riku could tell. Her hair was tied up in multiple braids and her eyes looked almost natural even with the sapphire glow to them. Riku cleared his throat.

"You want me to fight a woman?"

"Of course," Sagittarius replied. "It was she that plunged the Sword of Achilles into the trunk of the tree Ygdrasil. It was she that prevented the rot and fires from spreading throughout the countryside. It was she that last held that blade you now hold in your hands."

Riku looked down at the sword as he held it, and then at Yndvild. Even if nothing more than a revenant, her image gave off a mighty sense of courage. Riku awkwardly bowed and turned away to keep from blushing.

"Okay, do which one first?" he said and he resumed his rigid stance and readied his sword. This time Riku knew he saw Sagittarius smiling.

"All of them."

At once half a dozen legends came charging at Riku. He deflected the first attack, spun and blocked the second, then dodged the third. But then he felt a cold, sharp pain shoot into his hip that nearly sent him to the ground. He tried to turn but felt his body refuse to twist so long as the phantom blade remained stuck in him.

His attacker removed their blade and Riku could feel it go. He spun on his heels in anger and fear to see the cool, calm sapphire glow of Yngvild. She almost smiled and she plunged her sword into Riku's chest, driving him to the ground.

"Enough," Sagittarius said. In a split second each attacker was back at their position in the circle and Riku was gasping for air on the ground.

"What was that?! That hurt!" He cried as he rolled over and tried to stand.

"Your enemy will not wait for you to be ready. You must always be on your guard."

"But that was…that felt…" Riku pulled in air in great deep breaths.

"Real?" Sagittarius finished for him. "I would hope so. Your enemy is a devil with no mercy. He will toy with you, torture you, and skin you alive for his pleasure. He will send one hundred Dark Ones after you, knowing that you cannot win against five."

As Riku still sat on the ground, suddenly Sagittarius dismounted from his horse, dropped to one knee, and offered his hand. "What will you do? Will you die? Or will you cut them all down?"

Riku looked up, shocked that the archer had come down, literally, from his high horse for the first time since they met. He took the Zodiac's hand and stood up, gripping his sword tighter as he did.

"I understand," Riku nodded. "I'll do my best."

"Good," Sagittarius pulled off the face mask to reveal his burning eyes and approving smile. "Again!"

San Francisco was lost, and the Chaotic One, the Destroyer, Apollyon, relished in its demise. Slowly, he walked down the street with his arms held out at his sides while the buildings burned and the Dark Ones tore at steel and brick and flesh alike. This was a victory for him, just like in Paris, and he basked in the delight of it.

Apollyon laid his head back and stared up at the sky through the smoke, and he smiled bright for the camera. Half a dozen satellites honed in on the City by The Bay, desperately searching for an enemy, a target. But all they saw was one lone figure strolling casually through the destruction.

It made no sense to the US military top brass, nor to those at the Pentagon, or the President himself. All infrared cameras could pick up was the one target, but this couldn't have been done by one man. Live feeds from high altitude drones showed smoke and shadow, but no weapons, no army, no enemy except the one man.

The most advanced tracking systems in the world, the greatest available cameras and lenses that could be affixed to a satellite, capable of reading a license plate from two thousand kilometers away, were unable to detect the Dark Ones. And yet something, some *thing,* continually brought down any manned plane or helicopter that invaded what was now Apollyon's air space.

A blockade had formed around the city, with Alcatraz island becoming the new base of operations. The bridges were locked down, the ferries stopped, the roads on the south side of the city walled off. Most of the populace had escaped, but those that did couldn't explain what they saw or were too traumatized to speak at all.

As Apollyon mugged for the camera, a singular thought stabbed him in his side and stole his moment of victory. The Zodiac and their stewards had thwarted him just enough to save a precious few. Nearly half the city, as a matter of fact, escaped torture and death at the hands of Apollyon and his army. They achieved what hadn't been done in ages, and the thought made a very real chill creep down the Destroyer's spine.

How? He couldn't have told them. He can't, thought Apollyon. He closed his eyes and listened to the crackling of the fires, the crumbling of the buildings, the roaring of the torch that was the former Transamerica Pyramid. It was sweet music to his ears, and he soaked it in like a symphony. Then a violin struck a chord that was out of tune, a fly on the pages of his concerto.

His eyes opened and now it was all he could hear, the fly. No not one, dozens. Hundreds. Perhaps thousands, buzzing and swarming, twisting and….burned. Apollyon didn't exert the effort even to turn his head, but merely averted his gaze to one side and saw the approaching instrument of his annoyance.

The swarm of flies gathered near to the ground and quickly coalesced into the man, the Hat Man, Rezzek.

"*My massster,*" Rezzek hissed.

"You return from your task. I trust it went well." Apollyon snarled.

"*It did,*" Rezzek bowed lower.

"The curator?"

"*Dead.*"

"The tomes?"

"*If they ever existed…they are no more.*"

"Good. And the Healer?"

Rezzek pressed his forehead to the asphalt.

"*There were…complicationsssss.*"

Like a snake, Apollyon was on his quivering servant, with one hand on the back of his neck and the other on the ground. Rezzek's hat fluttered off by the gust of the quick movement and Apollyon positioned his lips a breath away from the deformed, gaunt ear of his servant.

"What...type...of...complications?!" His whisper may just as well have been the shout of one hundred men, as his voice beat into the Rezzek's ear. He shook and trembled with fear.

"The Zodiac! Ariesssss..."

"Should have been no problem whatsoever, given that you were carrying out *my* direct will!" Apollyon now shouted.

"The Healer...she tricked me...made it ssssseem like the plot...was my own!"

Apollyon's rage burned and the asphalt heated and began to melt under his hand. Acrid smoke from the tar and oil flooded all around Rezzek's face. Even for a being not quite alive, it was an unpleasant smell.

"So they found a loophole, hmm? These stewards are proving more resourceful than I care to admit. Still," Apollyon stood, picking Rezzek up as he did, and held him, dangling, in mid air.

High above them, another drone was torn from the sky by a Dark One that leapt effortlessly into the air. Its last image sent to the military base would be a blot of dark smoke covering it's camera lens before the feed was lost. Apollyon watched the creature and its prize plummet back to the ground and grinned.

"Still, this does make the game a bit more fun now, doesn't it?" He began to talk and walk, still holding Rezzek by the back of his neck.

"It doesss...master," Rezzek choked out the words as Apollyon squeezed his neck tighter.

"Now now, puppets don't speak," he gripped harder, his fingers almost tearing into Rezzek's throat. "What ever should I do? Throw you into the fire? Chop you up for spare parts? No, even the Wicked Man wouldn't accept a finger from such a failed experiment."

Apollyon tossed Rezzek like a piece of trash into the street and pointed a long boney finger at him.

"Perhaps the issue is such that you simply are no longer strong enough." With his other hand, Apollyon snapped and in moments Rezzek was surrounded by a dozen Dark Ones.

"Pleasssse master. Allow me to try...again. I will not fail you." Rezzek begged as he got to his knees.

"No," Apollyon smiled, "you most certainly will not. Not this time. Because if you do, I'll feed your soul to the Behemoth."

"No! Please I will not..."

Apollyon snapped his fingers again, cutting off Rezzek's pleas, and the Dark Ones surrounding him all gave a loud and ungodly howl. Each began to break apart, like pieces of used charcoal, drifting in the wind.

The dark ash shot out violently at Rezzek and seemed to penetrate his tattered clothes and gaunt skin. He threw his head back and cried out silently, his thin eyes open wide and the emptiness inside growing. His very form enlarged, the tattered clothes tore away and his gaunt skin grew black, leathery scales. Where fingers had been, rigid claws formed, even his teeth multiplied into tiny sharp yellow daggers.

Apollyon grinned at his new amalgamation.

"How do you feel now?" he asked.

Rezzek turned his gaze down towards his master, gone were the empty eye sockets, and stared at Apollyon with cat-like eyes that glowed a bright orange. He smiled, his mouth opened unnaturally wide and revealed row after row of monstrous teeth.

"*I am reborn,*" Rezzek said, his usual hiss far deeper than before.

"Good. Then find the Healer. Tear her to pieces. When you've done that, find the Prophet and bring him, mostly whole, to me."

Rezzek bowed low as Apollyon stepped forward and placed the black fedora back on his head.

"Go," he whispered.

Rezzek stood straight, his black duster split down the middle and shot out to both sides in the shape of giant wings. Rezzek leapt from the street and flew off to the East.

Apollyon laughed and looked out towards the bay.

"You see?! There is no hope. Send your machines of war! Do your worst! I, Apollyon, welcome it!"

Chapter 6

Jude stood on the edge of a grassy cliff, while clouds carried on a swift breeze swept by. He breathed in deep, while the sounds of birds on nearby branches reminded him of calmer days. The sun was warm on his face, which among the other sensations he felt was incredibly odd, since he wasn't really there.

In the distance, Jude could make out the sounds of people talking, exchanging goods and money. The noise rose up from the pavilions not far from where he stood, just beyond the walls and through the gate. He could almost make out what they were saying, but he wasn't really there.

He opened his eyes finally and took in the spectacular view. Wispy clouds and a great ocean of blue sky, and down below the cliff, far, far down below, the actual ocean. He stood on the edge of the floating city, Atlantis, as it glided perfectly balanced on air through the sky and towards its next port. But he wasn't really there.

"We have arrived," Taurus said as he sidled up next to Jude. "We are thirty days prior to the fall of Atlantis, just as you asked."

Jude turned to face Taurus and smiled.

"Thank you. I needed to see it, you know, before it crumbled and everyone died." Jude turned and walked away from the edge. He had been transported like before, back in time, very far back, to the lost City of Atlantis.

"What is it you need to see?" Taurus followed just over Jude's shoulder.

"I wanted to see...um, how they lived," Jude turned and forced a smile. "I wanted to see what it was like. Maybe if I can understand how they lived, and compare it with how we live now, I can have a better appreciation of the life I have, and, not take for granted anything before it's gone."

Even as the words stumbled out of his mouth, he knew it was complete gibberish. But he kept the smile long enough to turn around and hope Taurus bought at least some of it.

"I see," said the Zodiac after a moment. "Your failure in San Francisco has taught you a valuable lesson."

Jude fought the urge to turn and try to strangle Taurus to death. So instead he looked over his shoulder and grinned, nodding his agreement. He began to walk through the gate, hoping that he could ditch Taurus and go about his real purpose for being here.

"However," Taurus began again, to Jude's dismay, "I did warn you that you are not the leader."

"Oh yeah? And who is? Riku?"

"No, not Riku."

Thank goodness.

"You have not met the leader yet, but it will be the one called The Guardian."

"Who's charge is that supposed to be?" Jude was trying to hide his newfound interest in the topic. He stopped walking for a moment when he realized Taurus was standing still. "Something wrong?"

"No," Taurus sighed. "The answer to your question. Gemini, the Twins."

"The Twins? What about them?"

"The Twins are charged with finding The Guardian."

All of a sudden it dawned on Jude. He remembered that Taurus, for some reason he hadn't made clear, hated The Twins. Jude couldn't help himself and bent over, clutched his stomach and began laughing.

"Gemini?! You mean the two you hate?!"

Taurus rolled his eyes.

"I do not hate them. They are my family, after all."

"But you do! You totally do!" Jude reached out a hand to slap a passerby but his hand passed right through them.

"Hey look, man! Taurus has to deal with the two guys he hates!"

"I never said they were brothers. I said they were family." Taurus corrected.

"Wait, they're your sisters?"

"One of them. The Twins are brother and sister. Though they are quite inseparable we do not see eye to eye on...much." Taurus' look of disapproval at merely the mention of Gemini sent Jude into another fit of roaring laughter.

This was the distraction he needed. Anything to get Taurus willing to back off for an hour so he could go about his business. Jude kept up the laughter, to an obscene amount, even when he had to force himself to keep going. Taurus took another deep breath and began to look around aimlessly.

Perfect. Now.

"Look man, if you need to, I don't, know get some air or something before your favorite brother and sister show up, I'm sure I'll be fine," Jude said.

Taurus turned his eyes back on his charge and shrugged.

"I do not suppose you can accomplish too much trouble here. After all your body is in a safe place, even while your mind wanders."

The Zodiac was telling the truth about the safety of Jude's body. With the fresh attacks from the enemy, Taurus didn't want to take any chances. He had transported them both to an old wine cellar in Northern Italy.

The cellar, though filled wall to wall with sealed bottles, had belonged to a farmer who had died and forgotten to mention the vineyard in his will. Thus the cellar had not been disturbed in twenty years, and wouldn't likely be disturbed now that overgrowth completely covered the hard wood cellar doors on the far side of a dilapidated stone house. The odds of anyone finding them there, now, were astronomical.

"I think I will have a look around," Taurus said. "It has been ages, literally, since I've seen Atlantis. This..." he trailed off a moment before continuing. "This is a civilization I thought would have made it."

Taurus headed off in the direction Jude had wanted to go, waving a hand over his shoulder as he left.

"If you need me, you need but to think it."

And with that, Jude was finally alone. He breathed a heavy sigh and took off into the pavilions. Though he remembered seeing his target before in the common areas, he had a feeling things might be a little different now.

It was easy for Jude to weave through people, once he remembered they didn't really exist. At first he tried to be polite, even excusing himself as he nearly ran into them as they passed by. But then a small boy no higher than Jude's waist came barreling through the crowd, chased by another whom Jude assumed to be the boy's friend. Both children ran right through Jude as though either he or they were mere specters. It was a little unnerving.

After that, Jude wasted no more words or breath apologizing for walking directly through men and women alike. With his new found speed and with a renewed determination, he quickly made his way for what he assumed to be the government district of the city.

There were signs everywhere, but written in a language he could not read. Everyone was speaking to someone, but in a language he could not understand. So, he hurried towards the place where the men looked more important, wore better clothes, and had a look about them of pride and arrogance. In his own experience, politicians all shared at least that much in common.

Jude had a feeling that the man he had seen in the earlier vision, the man walking with Aquarius, must have been someone of importance. Taurus identified him as The Warrior of that age, but there was something about the man that was very different from the merchants he and Aquarius walked amongst. Although he couldn't quite remember the man's face, he knew there was something familiar. If only he could find the man and see him again, Jude was certain he'd recognize him.

"What are you doing here?"

Jude spun on his heels and came face to face, or rather face to chest with, Aquarius. He looked every bit the same as when he had visited Jude in the forest. His robes, his face, his hair, not a single hair out of place.

"Uh, I was just…I needed to…" Jude stammered, trying to come up with an excuse on the spot.

"You're quite lucky no one can see you. Nor I, for that matter." Aquarius began as he shook his head.

"Really I was just…" Jude tried to explain again, but then Aquarius walked forward and passed right through him.

Page 68

He swallowed hard and let out the breath he had held in. The Aquarius he ran into was the one of the past, not the one of his time.

"Have you come to check on them?" the voice behind Jude asked. A familiar voice, soft and playful but very, very familiar. Jude turned around and now looked at Aquarius' back, his body hiding the other man.

Then there was the language. Everyone in Atlantis spoke a language Jude could not understand. But Aquarius and this other man, he understood in perfect English. His curiosity piqued more, so he went to step around Aquarius, but just as he did, both men began to walk away and talk amongst themselves.

No, this was the precise reason he had made the journey back to this forgotten city. He had to know what Aquarius was up to with the other Warrior, and why this was to be his great downfall. Jude followed the men as they made their way out of the government district and into a lovely, ornate interior garden.

Aquarius sat down on a wrought iron bench and the other man did the same. They continued to talk, and Jude was quite sure they could not hear or see him, so he strode right up to them both.

It was the hair Jude saw first, the wispy, silver hair. His heart stopped in his chest, his lungs refused to work, his feet refused to go neither forward nor back. Aquarius laughed and carried on as though with his best friend, while Jude stood in shock and terror. It was him, sitting on the bench and bantering with Aquarius. It was Apollyon.

"Ya dinna say anythin' about climbing bloody frozen mountains in a bloody frozen wasteland!" Calleigh complained and she heaved in the arctic air. Leo stopped alongside her and grinned broadly under his beard.

"I thought you liked the cold?" He chuckled and produced a canteen from his belt that wasn't there moments ago. He handed it to Calleigh who nodded and took in long gulps of warm water.

"It's warm!"

"Wouldn't do much good if was cold, now would it?" Leo smiled and pointed just ahead of them. "There, just a few more meters and we'll have reached the saddle."

"Aye, and then what?" Calleigh handed the canteen back to Leo.

"Then we go in," Leo said as he began walking again.

"Go in? Go in where?!" Calleigh had to nearly jog just to catch up with Leo's great strides.

But he was right, within a few meters they both stood atop Mount Terror. Famed more for its use in science fiction novels and films, Mount Terror was the smaller of the two dormant volcanos on Ross Island. The view was nevertheless grand, as Calleigh took a moment to look in all directions. In most directions, there was nothing but white snow sitting on layers of ice. In another, she could clearly see Mount Erebus. But when she turned a bit, she could make out the vast ocean in the distance that stretched from the edge of the island to the horizon.

"It's beautiful," she said as she smiled and looked towards Leo. "Now get me somewhere warm 'fore I freeze my fingers off!"

Leo laughed and looked around at the top of the volcano.

"Ah ha! Here it is!" he explained as he jogged a short distance and brushed off a few inches of snow from a stone.

"That? That's a rock."

"And well hidden, too." Leo chuckled and smoothed off the top of the grey stone that jutted out of the surface inconspicuously. "What do you see?"

Calleigh looked around.

"I see snow."

"No no, look closer. The mountain. What do you see?"

"I dunno. Rocks, ice, snow."

"Yes, yes! Rocks. And what about them!?" Leo began to get excited.

"Hard stone, lava rock. Black and dense and probably old."

"Right. And what about this stone?" Leo pointed to the inconspicuous rectangle stone he had brushed off.

"I dunno. It's a rock. Grey and…"

"Exactly! Do you see any other stones the same color?"

Calleigh looked around as she pulled her jacket tighter around her. She didn't see any other stones the same color. Or any other color for that matter. While Mount Terror did have a decent amount of snow on it, the saddle where they stood was relatively free from it. And there wasn't another rock or outcropping anywhere she could see that had any other color than black.

She looked at the stone, roughly half a meter in length with the top surface area a little larger than a man's hand. Sure enough it was dark enough to be mistaken on first glance, but when examined closer it didn't match any kind of rock anywhere nearby. Calleigh shook her head as she tried to piece together the puzzle.

"I don't get it. Someone placed this here?"

Leo nodded, his smiled growing even larger.

"It won't respond to me. I'm not human. But if you put your bare hand on the top…" Leo motioned for her to touch the stone.

Calleigh raised an eyebrow, rolled her eyes and pulled the glove off her right hand.

"This better do somethin' or I swear to Mother Mary…" she placed her palm against the stone and was cut off mid sentence. She felt a jolt, like a small electric shock run up her arm, down her body and through he feet. It didn't hurt as much as it felt like something had just scanned her. She couldn't remove her hand from the surface of the stone, and suddenly her feet fell out from under her.

"Ah ha!" Leo laughed as they both fell through a large stone hatch, Calleigh's hand still attached to the stone. The hatch sprung closed over their heads as they came to a soft landing a few meters down. No, not a soft landing, a *slow* one. Something had slowed their fall and set their feet on sure footing.

"What in the name of St. Michael just happened?!" Calleigh looked around in the darkness. As if on cue, the walls around them began to buzz and came to life with cool blue light. Wide horizontal strips, one high and one low on each wall, illuminated the small square room in which they were standing, and the hallway before them.

"After you," Leo bowed and raised an arm. With the stone still attached to her palm, or rather her palm attached to the stone, she lead the way down the corridor. It wasn't long at all until they both came to an opening and a great, wide stone staircase. The staircase lead down and became wider as it went, opening the way into a massive underground cavern. As they walked a short way down the stairs, the ceiling opened up and shone with with the cool, blue light that illuminated a magnificent city.

"I, I can't believe it," Calleigh stammered as he eyes dazzled in the soft blue light. "Inside the volcano? What... what is this place?"

"I haven't seen this in ages," Leo looked about the perfectly preserved city and nodded his head in approval.

"You've been here!?"

"Yes, long long ago." Leo's smile began to fade. "Although I...I can't seem to remember."

"Ya, you've been havin' a lot o' that lately, haven't ya?" Calleigh said as she tried to take in the incredible view. "How come no ones been down 'ere? We can't be but a few dozen meters..."

"Two hundred, actually." Leo cut her off.

"What?!"

"We're just over two hundred meters below the point of entry. We fell a bit more than you realize, and the corridors are slanted downwards. Then there's the steps..."

"Alright, alright, I get it! What I don't understand is how this can be here. I mean, we are inside a volcano, right?"

"A volcano that's been dormant for a very, very long time." Leo said as he continued to walk down the grand staircase and towards the city.

"But someone would've found it by now," Calleigh once again had to pick up her pace just to keep up with Leo's long strides.

"Someone did find it. Several times throughout the years. The other stewards like you who fought against the Darkness. In your language, this place would be called the "City of Memory"," Leo chuckled a bit.

"What's funny?"

"It's a forgotten city, named 'Memory.' Memory!" Leo grabbed his gut and bellowed out a laugh that echoed down the stairs and throughout the giant domed cavern. Calleigh tried to hide her smile, but gave in and laughed as well.

"Aye, that is funny, I 'spose." Calleigh looked down at the stone that was still hanging from her palm. It didn't weigh her down, in fact it didn't seem to weigh anything. But just as it did not weigh on her arm, neither did it want to detach. As if reading her mind, Leo calmed his laughter, wiped his eye, and addressed it.

"Oh that. That would be the lantern," he said as he began to walk again. Calleigh followed. "You see, there was a guard posted at all times at the entrance, and he would be in charge of the lantern, the key into the city. With that you can access all the city's systems."

"Systems? What do you mean systems?"

"Like a computer. Only much, much, much more advanced than what you're used to."

"You mean like aliens and all that?" Calleigh asked, becoming even more intrigued. Leo sighed and shook his head.

"You humans are always so quick to think that someone else did all the work for you. Aliens built the pyramids. Aliens invented computers. Aliens abducted my mom," Leo frowned. "You're capable of a lot more than you think. It's that very reason Apollyon seeks to destroy you."

"Who now?"

"The Chaotic One, The Destroyer, Apollyon. His armies attacked Paris and San Francisco. He's your enemy, the reason I came to get you in the first place. Here we are," Leo said as they reached the bottom of the large staircase at last.

"And you want me to do what exactly? Kick him in the knee? Give him a firm talkin' to? You said his army destroyed those cities, so what can I do?" Calleigh asked while Leo lead her through a glowing maze of walls, openings and empty buildings.

"Oh there are others. Your teammates, and it's part of your job as The Purifier to assist them. That's where this place comes in."

"Right, I'll just purify people I've never met, from an underground city no one knows about. Right."

Leo smirked at Calleigh's constant attitude. Then his smile quickly faded as they entered what would be the basement of what would've been a very important room. Leo stared in both disbelief and anger, at a bronze vat roughly one meter tall and half a meter in diameter. It sat in the middle of the room, otherwise empty, and looked like it hadn't been touched for centuries.

"What...what's that?" Calleigh asked, breaking the silence.

"That, is the reason we've come here. An artifact missing for ages. It was created by one of my own, and then it vanished one day. I thought it was lost but recently found out it was not lost, just hidden."

"By who?" Calleigh stepped closer to it, admiring the craftsmanship.

"One who betrayed us, I see. My brother Aquarius." Leo stepped to the other side opposite Calleigh and motioned her to come near. She obeyed and the moment she did the lantern dropped from her hand and landed firmly in the sand by her feet.

"Here, place your hands on the edge, like so," Leo demonstrated. "This is the Cistern. An artifact of immense and incredible power. With this, you will be able to complete your charge and help save this world."

Calleigh gently laid her hands on the Cistern and gasped in amazement as it began to fill with water from the bottom up. She hadn't noticed any openings in it, but the water rose steadily towards the top. As it did, the Cistern itself began to glow, the bronze appearing to heat up but she couldn't feel any heat emitting from it.

"Your Earth is made of water, from the oceans to the lakes to rivers, above and under the ground. Even this continent is covered in ice, frozen water. With the Cistern, you can do many things, but most important you can communicate with the other stewards. Together you are an army, meant to fight against Apollyon."

"I'm not a fighter, I'm a archaeologist. I dig up old things and pack 'em away and find more old things. I don't fight." Calleigh's eyes widened as she stared into the swirling water within the Cistern.

"All armies have orders. All armies communicate. Apollyon seeks to disrupt communication within the ranks of the human armies but with the Cistern, that communication between the stewards is unbreakable." Leo's voice began to get lower, stronger, resonating through the room as he spoke.

"But I haven't even met them." Calleigh replied.

"Then it's time you do." Leo smiled.

Chapter 7

Samantha looked around her apartment and gave a great sigh as she collapsed into her favorite, and only, chair in the living room. It had been only a few days since she left here for work and had not come back, but it seemed like months had passed, given the recent events. Except for the stack of mail by the front door that had accumulated over the last few days, most of which were bills, not much had really changed. It was almost as though she had simply gone on a little vacation.

There were of course other signs of her absence. Though she had carried her mobile phone with her throughout the trip, her service plan did not include international coverage. So her excursions with Aries to various parts of Africa meant she was not receiving the multiple phone calls, emails, and text messages from her work and coworkers wondering where she was. Samantha's return to the United States by way of San Francisco also didn't help her connectivity, since once the attacks began on the city, all cellular signals became blocked by the supernatural presence of the Dark Ones.

Now as she tried to relax and felt the exhaustion truly kick in, rest would seem impossible with her phone updating and alerting her to every one of those missed calls and messages.

"You are quite popular," Aries commented as she stared out the window to the city.

"Yeah about that," Samantha groggily picked up her phone and began dismissing alerts. "Just work wondering why I haven't shown up for my shift. Where I went, when I'm coming in. Blah blah blah." She looked closer and shook her head with a grunt.

"What is it?" Aries asked as she turned from the window.

"Not one single 'hey hope you're ok Sam' message to be found. Just a bunch of threats of losing my job. Guess no one watches the news, huh?"

Aries opened the window and in came Buddy, screaming and howling as though he hadn't been fed in years.

"Oh my gosh I'm so sorry, Buddy!" Samantha ran to the window and scooped up the angry black cat in her arms. She rocked him as she went to the kitchen and grabbed one, then another, can of wet cat food. She set Buddy down on the floor and peeled back the lid of the first can. No sooner had she set it down than he dove in face first.

"That's right, big boy. At least you're still a part of my normal life." Samantha opened the other can and left it by the cat, then returned to her chair and plopped back down.

Aries moved closer and knelt by the chair. Even so, she was still as tall as Samantha had she been standing next to the Zodiac.

"It is not so much as that," Aries gently placed a hand on Samantha's arm. "The Chaotic One brings death, destruction, fear and turmoil. But eventually, all will cease to remember his presence, as well as everything he has done."

At this, Samantha suddenly sat up straight, incensed.

"You guys keep mentioning that. So you're saying all these people that have died, all these cities that will burn, no one will even remember them?"

"In time, future generations will find clues of their existence, but the memories of what happened, or how it happened, where these civilizations went, will all be gone. How is it you think the Mayans disappeared without a trace?"

"Or Atlantis, like Jude said, yeah." Samantha breathed in deep, her eyebrows furrowed as she tried to think. "I just don't get it. I don't understand why this is happening."

"Understanding why is not the goal," Samantha looked up at Aries who was now smiling, now beaming with light. "Preventing it in the first place is. Fighting to protect that which you as a people have accomplished, and creating a stronger, better future. That is the goal."

Samantha looked into Aries' eyes, she could have gotten lost in them for the depth, and tried to find the answer she was looking for. She swallowed hard and shook her head, giving in to the fact that the mysteries of the universe might not be solved in an afternoon in her living room.

"But you said that none of us have ever defeated Apollyon," Samantha finally said.

Aries' smile did not fade, her countenance did not diminish as she answered. "Just because it has not been done, does not mean it cannot be done."

Samantha nodded her understanding and got up from her chair. She immediately regretted not resting more but there was work to be done. She pointed to the four velvet bags lying on the floor and turned to Aries.

"Okay, how about you help me translate whatever is written on those things? Maybe there's some clue left behind on how to beat this bastard before he takes out another city."

Samantha knelt on the floor and opened the first bag. Each tablet was solid gold, heavy, and probably priceless. Making the tablets out of gold was a good idea, because like

Aries had pointed out earlier, gold does not rust. Writing on the tablets in blood was another matter all together, because as Samantha knew from her medical training, blood can be washed off.

Such was the case with the former Prophet's tomes. Still, Samantha laid them all out in what seemed like a logical order on her floor, and with Aries' help tried to decode what was written long ago. How these tomes ever ended up in the hands of the Egyptian curator would be a mystery unsolved, for as they quickly found out, the story contained on the tablets was of the fall of Yggdrasil, the Viking city in America, and the betrayal of one of their own.

As they began to read through and piece together the details of what had happened, Samantha ended up shifting a few tablets in order to make the continuity of the story flow a little better. There were no names given, but mentions of "Guardian", "Warrior", and "Healer" were plenty. It was like they were more than just a group of random people, but actually family, or so Samantha thought.

The author spent more time describing the events that lead up to the destruction of their civilization than anything else. He detailed their preparation and the things that worked against the Dark Ones, versus the things there were of no effect. His main focus was on two central characters, though, that seemed almost at odds from the beginning. The Guardian, whom Samantha knew was Rezzek, and The Warrior.

She noticed something as she read along, or rather as Aries translated for her. The Prophet of that time seemed to do nothing more than record and catalog events as they happened. But there didn't appear to be any actual prediction of future events, people or places. Furthermore, there was absolutely no attempt, like Jude, to alter the events using the very words he was writing. The author just seemed to jot down how things happened, where they ended up, and then very abruptly the story stopped.

"I guess that's where he died," Samantha said as she sat back on her heels.

"Yes," Aries replied, "he passed in his home while the city burned. Before The Warrior stopped the flames that engulfed the great tree. She plunged her sword into the center of the trunk and turned the tree, trunk, roots and all, into stone."

"Wait, her sword? Is that the same sword Riku was swinging around?"

"It is."

"Wow, he's literally holding history." Samantha marveled.

"No different than your armband," Aries pointed out. "Worn by the queen Cleopatra."

Things had been so crazy Samantha hardly noticed that she still had the armband on. She went to remove it and give her arm a rest but then thought better of it. She looked up at Aries and pointed out the tablets.

"So why didn't he do what Jude did? Why didn't he try to change things?"

"Your Prophet discovered his abilities, but not all do. The same goes for the Healers, the Guardians, and the Purifiers. Not all stewards grasp the full range of their abilities."

"But if we did?"

Aries smiled.

"You *would* save this world."

Samantha grinned back, a plan forming in her head. Buddy strode up to her and rubbed his face against her leg, purring his forgiveness for her absence. She rubbed the cats head and let her mind drift into thought for a few minutes, the only sound being that of the purring cat.

But her thoughts were cut short as her apartment began to rumble. Buddy hissed loudly and bolted for the window, disappearing through it while Samantha carefully made her way to a hallway door frame and braced herself as the tremors increased in strength.

"Aries…New York doesn't have earthquakes like this!" Samantha shouted as the ground churned beneath her building. Aries nodded, her demeanor changed to let Samantha know who was behind it. She marched towards Samantha but before she could reach her, the floor between the two erupted as a massive black cloud filled the room, the force of the impact knocking Aries back and out the window.

"Aries!" Samantha shouted. A dark, malevolent voice began laughing from the dark cloud, and swirled and twisted in her apartment.

"*Hello again…Sssssssamantha!*" Rezzek hissed.

Jude held his breath, or preformed the act of doing so, as he carefully followed Aquarius and Apollyon. They walked casually through the streets of Atlantis, chatting and laughing with one another like old friends. It burned Jude to think that Aquarius would have the gall to ask a favor of him, knowing that once upon a time he so blatantly strolled with the sworn enemy of the Zodiac; of humanity itself.

He tried his best to listen in on what was being said, but he noticed that this visit into the past somehow also muffled voices. Not just any voices, but specifically the voices of Aquarius and Apollyon. Maybe it was because this vision was being seen through the memories and eyes of Taurus that things weren't entirely clear. It could be that if Taurus didn't witness or hear everything directly, his recollection would be askew. Then a truly terrifying thought entered into Jude's mind.

The first time he had visited Atlantis, he and Taurus saw Aquarius walking with a man through the courtyard. Aquarius looked up and saw Taurus but there was no sign of admissions of guilt. What if Taurus couldn't *see* Apollyon at all? He knew Apollyon somehow made people forget, so what if he was in league with Aquarius and the other Zodiac were none the wiser?

Jude looked up from his thoughts and panicked. He had stopped to contemplate and completely lost track of the two he was following. Quickly he jogged through the sea of people, literally through, trying to relocate them. He stopped short suddenly when he saw, towering over the crowd, the horns on top of Taurus' forehead.

He quietly sank back in amongst the people, hoping Taurus hadn't yet noticed him. He needed more time to try and figure out what Aquarius was up to, and he knew once Taurus got involved things would just fall apart.

Jude turned and quickly headed back the way he came, when he nearly ran into the wispy silver hair of his recent tormentor. He paused in fear, fear that Apollyon would turn and face him. Fear that he would grind his face into the cobblestone. Fear that he would laugh that terrifying laugh that somehow reached into Jude's soul.

But the Chaotic One neither turned nor paid Jude any mind as he and Aquarius continued to walk.

"You really…will be able to…presence of my forces…" Jude heard Apollyon say. He doubled his efforts in following this time, opting not to be distracted by anything.

"How many ages have…this?" Aquarius answered.

"How many…have there been?" Apollyon chuckled.

Jude walked through the pair and turned to face them, walking backwards as he needed to try and read their lips when the voices were muffled.

"But honestly," Aquarius continued, "even without the use all twelve artifacts, the stewards are themselves, weapons."

"Maybe. Does that mean you're willing to take my wager?" Apollyon flashed a mischievous grin.

"We wouldn't be talking otherwise. But you do know my terms as well."

"Oh yes, yes. The other Zodiac are not to know about our arrangement."

"And?" Aquarius stopped walking, his face became more serious.

"And what?" Apollyon shrugged. Aquarius squinted his eyes, clearly not amused.

"Right, right. And if you win, I will take leave for a millennia. Mankind will be free to do whatever it is those filthy apes do."

"You would be do well to remember those filthy apes have outsmarted you on more than one occasion." Aquarius began walking again.

"But not every time, Zodiac. Not every time," Apollyon grinned.

Jude stopped for a moment to think, while still keeping an eye on the two as they strolled into a very open and very empty courtyard. Outsmarted Apollyon? But Taurus, Aries, even Sagittarius told them all that mankind had never won. That Apollyon has destroyed every great civilization the world has ever own, and has been unmatched in doing so. Now he *knew* something was wrong with their memories, if they couldn't recall a single victory.

Jude sat down on a hard bench, he didn't think he needed to hear much more, but he would continue following and listening as long as he could anyway. He already knew the outcome of Atlantis, it would be destroyed and the stewards would fail in their attempts at stopping the Darkness. He need-ed a plan. He needed to ensure all twelve artifacts were found and put to use.

And he needed to find Taurus, to see if he could recog-nize Apollyon in this vision of the past.

Samantha could feel what felt like thousands of bugs crawling all over her skin as a massive black hand pinned her back against the wall of her apartment. It squeezed her arms and she was afraid if it kept this up her ribs would crack. The dark enlarged specter that was Rezzek laughed from every-where, and the noise shook the walls and floor of the place.

"Get...off...me!" Samantha managed to shout.

"Or what? What will you do? What can *you do?!"* Rezzek laughed again. Suddenly Samantha found herself hurled through the air as he tossed her like a rag out the same window from which Aries had plummeted. She didn't have enough time to think, to catch a breath or react at all. She didn't even see her life flash before her eyes as her body flew down a few stories to the street below.

"I have you!" Aries exclaimed as she caught Samantha just a few meters from the asphalt and lowered her gently to her feet. Samantha nodded an unspoken thanks and turned her gaze back up to the apartment.

"We have to get these people out of here. He's going to cause so much destruction just trying to kill me."

"No, you need to run. I will slow him, you get to safety."

"I...I can't do that, Aries." Samantha swallowed hard as an explosion rocked the upper floors of the building, followed by maniacal laughter. "This is my job, right? I'm the Healer."

"The Healer need not fight. I can summon Sagittarius and the Warrior. It is his charge to..."

Another explosion rocked the entire block, and something came crashing down through the floors of the building, sending glass and brick and dust pouring out the bottom floor. A moment later, Rezzek stepped out of a new hole in the wall, his body solid once more, but much different than Samantha had seen prior.

He still wore the hat, and a tattered duster, but the rest of his visage was completely unrecognizable. His body was no longer made of gaunt, withered flesh that hung to a skeletal frame. Gone were the black, empty eye sockets and shrunken nose. Now his face looked, for lack of a better word, puffy.

His arms were bulging with unnatural muscles that had burst out of his clothing. His legs and chest looked the same, like some body builder on too many steroids.

When Rezzek breathed, Samantha could smell rot and sulfur. It was enough to make her want to puke, and nothing made her *want* to puke. He stepped closer one slow step at a time, savoring the victory he was ensured to have this time.

"I have pondered how I would kill you, Healer. Ssssso many different ways. Break your bones, tear your limbssss off. Destroy your mind first, yes yes. But I think instead, I'll sss-simply eat your soul."

Samantha looked up at Aries, suddenly very concerned.

"Can he do that? Can he eat my soul?"

"He has been, altered. Empowered, by Apollyon. I will call the Warrior." Aries looked to the sky and raised her left arm high.

"I think not!" Rezzek shouted, swung his arm out and a chunk of debris hopped right over Samantha and crashed into Aries, knocking her back into the adjacent building. Samantha gasped as Aries disappeared in the rubble.

"You know what?" She turned to Rezzek. "Yea, go ahead, eat my soul. I hope you choke on it!" Samantha charged forward, her bare foot stepping into a new puddle of water from the broken pipes up above. She had a split second to ponder where she lost her shoe, but determined it didn't matter.

"Hello? Are you…are you the Healer?" Came a voice from everywhere. Samantha looked around at her surroundings and saw that time itself seemed to have stopped.

"Um, hi?" She replied.

"Bloody hell, it worked! It worked Leo!...Ya, ya I know. Hi there, I'm Calleigh. I'm 'spose to be your Purifier."

"Ok, uh hi. How are you doing this?" Samantha soon realized though she could talk, none of her other motor functions were working. She, too, was frozen in time.

"Uh, doin' what? Talkin'? I'm in some ancient city under the ice in Antarctica." Calleigh said.

"Antarctica?!"

"Yeah I know, right? Look this tall fella told me a bunch o' stuff and said I was supposed to help you out."

"Calleigh, was it? Look I'm about to have my soul eaten. It was nice to meet you but..."

"Yer soul eaten!?"

There was silence for a few moments. Then the voice came back.

"Okay, now you listen to me. We just met and I dinna climb up a bloody frozen volcano to have my new warrior partner or whatever ya are get her soul eaten! You tell me how to help, an' I'll do it!"

Samantha thought as quick as she could. She could feel the air around her moving again, very slowly but she felt like time was catching up. If there were new players on the board, maybe she could survive this attack yet.

"Jude! Contact Jude! Uh...the Prophet! I don't know how you're doing what you're doing but get the Prophet on the...voice, air thing. Tell him I'm fighting Rezzek! The Hatman!"

"Right. Jude, Prophet, Hatman. Got it. Be back in a jiffy!"

Suddenly time was back to normal and Samantha found herself barreling towards Rezzek. She closed her eyes and clenched her fists as tight as she could. Maybe she would land a lucky blow.

Instead, Samantha felt an incredible force land on her jaw. The impact was so powerful, she thought her neck might snap as her head twisted over her shoulder and carried the rest of her body behind it to crash onto the rubble that had landed on Aries. The pain wasn't immediate, most likely from the shock of the impact.

When she opened her eyes again, Samantha saw Rezzek's left arm still in the position of a powerful left hook. If her jaw wasn't completely shattered, she would be very surprised indeed. She tried to move but her right leg wouldn't respond. It was twisted in an ungodly direction that made her wince when she saw it. So she grit her teeth, placed her shaking hands on her right thigh, and held her breath.

Heal, dammit!

A shock went from the palm of her hands, into her leg and down out her toes. The leg slowly turned back into the proper position, complete with the sounds of crunching bones and pounded meat, and then was back to normal.

With a heavy grunt, she forced herself to her feet and turned her eyes back to Rezzek. The right side of her face was already swelling and the pain had started to kick in. It was a terrible, fiery pain that grew and grew with each moment her heart beat. She knew if she didn't do something fast she'd pass out.

"I did not expect ssssuch fight from you, Healer!" Rezzek laughed. He moved closer slowly, his footsteps shook the ground, as though his very body mass had increased one hundred fold.

"I'm...not dead...yet," Samantha stammered from the left side of her mouth.

"I will fix that for you," Rezzek picked up speed, clearing the distance between them in a few strides. He pulled his right arm back to finish her, when the rubble behind Samantha exploded and out shot Aries with a blow of her own.

"Demon!" Aries shouted, her fist crashing into Rezzek and knocking him two blocks down the street.

"You need to flee, Healer!" Aries said to Samantha. Fleeing did sound like a good idea, but she was certain if she tried to move now, she would simply crash to the ground in pain.

"Aries…someone contacted me…Calleigh…said she was…the Purifier." Samantha's entire right side of her face was swelling fast, her right eye almost swollen shut and she was losing the ability to speak.

"Contacted you?" Aries' eyes went wide. "Time…did time slow to a halt?"

Samantha nodded slowly. She was losing consciousness.

"The Cistern has been found! Then hope has been restored!"

A deep guttural laughter began resonating from down the street, it carried to where they were standing and seemed to surround them.

"Hope? Foolishness! Come, Healer, it's time to die!"

Samantha sighed, her vision blurred from the incredible pain in her face. She couldn't fight it anymore, and she began to fall to the ground. Aries quickly reached down and caught her as she faded fast. She placed Samantha's hand over her right cheek and held it there. In the distance, she could hear the footsteps of Rezzek as he strode towards them. Samantha's left eye shut while her body went limp in Aries' arms.

Heal...heal...

"Taurus! Hey, Taurus where are you?" Jude called out. He had climbed up on one of the walls that overlooked the courtyard. He wouldn't let Aquarius out of his sight, not this time, and he wanted to test his theory that Taurus would not be able to recognize Apollyon. Taurus hadn't before, when he identified the man walking with Aquarius to be the Warrior of that age.

"C'mon man, where are you?"

"Here," Taurus said from across the other side of the courtyard.

"Hey, I want to show you something. Meet me over here in this courtyard." Taurus nodded in agreement and began walking towards Jude. This was it, he would get some answers and finally figure out what Aquarius had done.

Atlantis was known to the Zodiac as the great failure of their brother. As far as anyone knew, the fall of the floating city was enough to drive Aquarius into a great despair that even lead to his self exile. But if Jude was right, it wasn't the fall of the city that was his failure, it was a failed wager. Jude knew somewhere in his heart that Apollyon had cheated, and the result was the utter destruction of what he saw as one of the greatest human achievements in history.

Jude hopped down from the wall and eagerly waited for Taurus to catch up. Aquarius and Apollyon hadn't moved from their bench and were still embroiled in conversation. Everything was going perfectly according to Jude's plan.

"'Ello there. Are you Jude?" came a voice that filled the air. Jude tried to spin around and see who was talking but his body was frozen in time. He looked out the corner of his eye and saw Taurus, too, was frozen.

What is this?!

"Ya are the Prophet, aren't ya?" the voice said again.

"Um...yes. Who's speaking?"

"Oh thank the maker, I'm Calleigh! I'm your Purifier!" Calleigh said, jubilantly.

"Oh. Okay. How are you doing this to..."

"Never mind 'cause I dunno. But look see, your Healer, well *our* Healer, is havin' her soul eaten by someone called Hatman. She told me to find you, 'cause you would know what to do."

No no not now! I'm right here! I need to know! Jude thought.

"Um, Calleigh, can you freeze time like this on Samantha?"

"I dunno what I can do! I climbed up a bloody frozen volcano, and now I'm in this ancient city with this tall Zodiac hunk o' man who keeps pacing and giving me th' eye. And Samantha said she needs your help, so you're gonna help her, or so help me I'll..."

"Okay, calm down. We'll deal with the how and why and all that later. You're the Purifier?"

"Aye," Calleigh said, tension obviously in her voice.

"What does the Purifier do?"

"How should I know!?"

"You said one of the Zodiac was there with you? Ask him. It's important."

There was silence for a few moments, meanwhile nothing moved. Jude tried to will his muscles to move but nothing would happen. Suddenly he became very aware of water, somewhere around his hand. Maybe his hand was in water. He couldn't tell exactly but he knew there was water somewhere.

Then the vision all around him began to grow hazy, like a waking up from a dream. Jude panicked, he looked left and right still unable to move. The walls of the city turned to blurred, puffy clouds, the street beneath his feet began to fade into cold, damp mud. Something was pulling him out of the vision.

"Calleigh! Are you doing this?! Hey c'mon now, whatever you're doing I need you to stop!" His own words echoed in his brain, no longer real words but thoughts that swirled in his mind. He took one last look at Aquarius and Apollyon, and swore that he saw Apollyon look directly into his eyes, and smile.

Jude took a sharp gasp of air and found himself sitting on the damp floor of the wine cellar in Italy. His right hand lay limp at his side in a small puddle of water.

"No no no! Oh c'mon!" Jude tried to stand but found he was still frozen in time.

"Right, so…" came Calleigh's voice from everywhere and nowhere.

"Calleigh! I need you to send me back!" Jude exclaimed.

"Back? I dunno where ya were? Look, are ya gonna help Samantha or not?"

Jude grit his teeth and would've clenched his fists if he could've moved. The vision was gone, it didn't mean he couldn't go back. But right now, his teammate needed help. Jude wracked his brain trying to think of a solution. The only thing that came to mind was…

"You're the Purifier, right?"

"Aye."

"Reach Samantha, however you're doing this. Get a hold of her fast. I have an idea."

"Finally! Oh and uh, it's nice to meet you, by the way."

"Yeah," Jude sighed, "you too."

Chapter 8

Riku sat crosslegged on the cool grass in the middle of a large field. His sword stuck in the ground next to him as he tried dialing, again, any of his fellow stewards. It was dark in Japan, a cloudless sky overhead gave the perfect view of the stars and galaxies in the great distance. He knew that it was surely daytime wherever Jude and Samantha were, so the fact they didn't answer his calls could only mean one thing.

They were busy.

They were dead.

Two things. It meant two things.

Riku shook the idea of of his mind that they were dead, because surely Sagittarius would have said something by now if that were the case.

"I cannot reach my brethren," Sagittarius, as if reading Riku's mind, stepped forward and said. "There is much activity among the Dark Ones, and this makes my connection to the others...difficult."

"That doesn't mean they're dead," Riku jumped to his feet.

"Dead? No, not at all." Riku breathed a sigh of relief. "Dying perhaps, but not yet dead."

"What are we waiting for then!? Let's go help them!"

"It is better for you to continue to train. When the time comes you must be ready to face numerous opponents at once. Are you ready?"

Riku sat back down in the grass and tossed his phone. He felt ready, from the first day Sagittarius walked into his dojo, he felt ready. When he helped Samantha in Africa, he felt ready, and when he fought the Dark Ones in the underground of San Francisco, he felt ready. So why should he keep practicing and training when among all the other two members of his group, he was the most ready.

Surprisingly, Sagittarius sat down in the grass beside Riku. He hadn't seen the Zodiac sit at all, unless on top his horse that is. Now he sat back on his heels, knees bent beneath him, and looked more samurai than he ever had before. Riku had a quick thought to fetch his phone and take a picture, but Sagittarius spoke up.

"For ages we have watched you humans, and interacted only when necessary. We have stayed back and let history run its course, and let you discover your potential on your own," he sighed and reached up to remove his face mask. "When the age is over and the Darkness has come and gone, we return to our posts on the edge of space and watch. What else do you think we do?"

Riku looked up and him and shrugged.

"I don't know. What is there to do on the edge of space?"

"We sulk. We regret. We reflect. What did we do wrong? What could we have done better? Will anyone but us remember the names of the fallen?"

Sagittarius hung his head and stared at the grass. Riku kept an eye on him, watching this mighty samurai turn almost human in emotion, at least.

"What would you do differently?" Riku asked, barely above a whisper.

"I would tell my charge, my steward, to save one city."

Page 98

"Just one?"

"Just one. One city saved from the Darkness, saved from being forgotten for all time. One city allowed to advance and to grow. I feel that, if not for our great failure, many other cities would have flourished." It looked to Riku as though Sagittarius was staring far off into the past, looking at those long lost civilizations.

"Why only one? Why not the whole world?"

Sagittarius smiled, actually smiled.

"How many do you think there needs to be, to remember the rest?" With that he got back to his feet, towering over Riku. "Come, Warrior. Let us train."

Riku got back up and brushed himself off.

One city. Save one city. Riku smiled to himself.

Samantha groggily opened her eyes, both of them, and looked up at the mighty Aries, who still held her in one arm. With the other arm, Aries held out her golden dagger, a large flaming ram's head protruding from the blade and posted a few meters in front of them. Samantha glanced to one side and saw Rezzek, massive as ever, beating against the flaming ram and laughing as he did so.

She looked down and saw a steady stream of water trickling past them and noticed the source, a broken fire hydrant across the street. Prying her own hand off her cheek, which was healed but still somewhat sore, Samantha laid her arm back and touched a single finger to the stream of water.

Time stopped.

"Healer? Bloody hell, there ya are!" Calleigh shouted from everywhere.

"Hey Calleigh," Samantha replied weakly.

"I got Jude on the…phone? I 'spose, I don't really know how all this works. But anyway, he's here."

"Samantha?" Jude's voice came through loud and clear.

"Hey, what's up?"

"Our new friend says you're in trouble. What's the situation?"

"The situation? Geez you're a nerd," Samantha cleared her throat. "Rezzek is on some dark steroids or something. He nearly knocked my head off with one punch. Aries is holding him back but it look like she's slipping."

"I have an idea," Jude appeared to not have even listened to a word she said. Samantha rolled her eyes.

"Fine, let's hear it."

"Calleigh, you're the Purifier. But you don't know what that means, right?"

"Oh aye," Calleigh answered, somewhat indignantly.

"And Samantha, you're the Healer. You heal *people*."

"And plagues, don't forget plagues," Samantha felt her sarcasm coming back with each breath.

"What if there's still some human left in Rezzek? What if you could heal the taint in him, like you did in Africa with that diamond, and Calleigh you could…I don't know…purify the evil out of him?"

"You mean, turn him back to a plain old human?" Samantha asked, the plan beginning to make more sense.

"Exactly! And then kill him of course. But we'll get to that…"

"Wait a minute," Calleigh interjected. "I dunno how I'm doing what I'm doing. I dunno how to *purify* anythin'."

"You'll figure it out, I believe in you." Jude replied quickly.

"That means he's pulling this out of his ass, Calleigh." Samantha noticed the fiery ram flicker, and reverberations from Rezzek's hits began to move once again. "Look guys, I'm out of time here. If we're going to try this, we need to do it now."

"Calleigh! You have a Zodiac there with you. Ask him!" Jude shouted.

Time retuned to normal, and Rezzek's strikes began to blow bits and pieces of the ram off in all directions.

"Aries!" Samantha yelled, drawing the Zodiac's attention.

"Fantastic, you live!"

"Yeah, sorta. Listen, I need you to get me close to Rezzek. I need to…touch him."

"You will likely die, Healer."

"Maybe. But I need to try."

Aries nodded and lowered her dagger, the ram vanished and Rezzek cracked his neck and smiled.

"*Accepting your fate, I ssssee!*" Rezzek hissed.

"Here goes," Samantha stood up, almost falling over as the blood rushed from her head. "You want my soul? Fine. I'm sick of you anyway." She stumbled forward a few steps, looking down to see where the water on the street was.

"*Good! Now kneel before me!*"

Samantha rolled her eyes, spotted a puddle, and knelt down with her knees resting in the water.

"This had better work, Jude," she whispered to herself. "Or I'm haunting your skinny ass."

Page 101

Jude tugged off one shoe and his sock and stepped in the wettest part of the cellar. Taurus, excitedly, had told him how the Cistern worked with water to connect the stewards. He pulled his notebook from his bag and began to furiously write.

"The Zodiac...beaming with pride...instructed Calleigh the Purifier...on what to do." He spoke as he jotted down words.

"The Cistern has been lost to us for ages," Taurus smiled. "To know that is has returned only means..."

"Yes, yes, I get it. Look, we need Riku. Can you do that mind thing you do and get Sagittarius? We need him to be wherever Samantha is in like, two minutes."

Taurus nodded. "It will be done."

Jude turned back to his notebook and stared intently at the words.

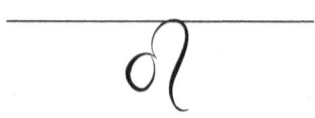

"I'm very proud of you, Purifier," Leo said, his arms crossed over his chest, a look of approval across his face.

"Sure, thanks," Calleigh said, her hands plastered to the edges of the Cistern, as she nervously rocked back and forth. "So what exactly do I do now?

"If the Prophet's plan works, the three of you will cleanse that abomination and put him to rest, permanently."

"But *how* exactly? I dunno how I'm supposed to purify anythin'! I'm still new to this, ya know."

Leo nodded and stepped forward.

"They're all still connected?"

"Aye, I can…see and…feel those two. Bloody strange, if ya ask me."

"Good. Now, watch carefully. Right when you feel the time is right, plunge your hand into the Cistern!" Leo moved even closer, his eyes wild with excitement.

"Oooookay," Calleigh said nervously, looking into the swirling water of the Cistern. Without another word or second guess, she removed her right hand from the side of the Cistern and shoved it into the water.

The water shot out of the Cistern in a massive torrent and surrounded both her and Leo in and instant. It filled the room to the ceiling while Leo laughed madly. Then the scene changed completely. No longer was she huddled in a room in the lost city of Memory, but instead she stood on a street she'd never seen before.

Calleigh looked around quickly to see that Leo, the Cistern, everything was gone and replaced with this strange place. Suddenly, a woman came into view, frozen in time but on her knees looking upward. Then the giant, dark frame of a monster, towering over the woman and grinning down at her, materialized before her eyes.

"Samantha?" Calleigh slowly approached. "Is that you?"

"Calleigh? You ready?" Samantha spoke without moving.

"Aye. I dunno how, but let's give this a whirl."

"Just...please don't get me killed. Okay?"

Calleigh nodded, not realizing that Samantha couldn't see her as she did.

"Ready when you are, love." Calleigh voice trembled. She moved closer and stood right next to Samantha. Then, for reasons she couldn't understand, she felt herself reach out and place a hand on Samantha's shoulder.

Time moved forward as she stood there, in awe as she felt like she was actually there in New York with the Healer. Calleigh quickly crossed herself with her other hand.

"Mother Mary..."

Samantha could feel a hand on her shoulder, though no one was standing next to her. She could feel the worried eyes of Aries on her back, as the Zodiac stood, somewhat powerless behind her. She turned her gaze up to Rezzek and grimaced.

"Get it over with, you bastard," Samantha growled.

"*With...pleasure!*" Rezzek growled and hunched over, his mouth opening twice as wide as natural. Within his throat, Samantha could see, no feel, pain and eternal suffering. She was paralyzed and felt like she couldn't breathe. She felt a hot, rotting wind tugging on her very being. It felt like torture; it felt like dying.

With a loud scream, Samantha forced herself to raise both hands and grab the sides of Rezzek's face. He shut his mouth out of pure surprise and stared at her with cold burning eyes.

"All right you bastard," Samantha growled. "*Heal!*"

She felt the invisible hand on her shoulder grip her tight, and the electric shock she had become accustomed to multiplied ten fold. She could feel the squirming, rotting flesh of Rezzek's face in her hands burn and somehow scream, like the skin itself was alive independently of the monster.

"It's working!" Jude shouted from everywhere.

Samantha could hear a woman shouting what sounded like a battle cry in Gaelic, and only assumed it was Calleigh. Rezzek howled loud and terrible, his voice carried down the streets and shattered windows of parked cars and apartments alike. Samantha held on, and before her eyes, chunks of ash and rotted flesh fell to the ground.

A great burst of light shot out from her hands, and threw Samantha and Rezzek back in opposite directions. Aries caught Samantha, and she felt the mysterious hand vanish from her shoulder.

"Did we...did we?" Samantha managed to utter.

"Look and see," Aries pointed out.

Lying on the ground, half covered in blackened mud, was a thin, frail man with light colored long hair and a blonde goatee. He coughed and groaned in pain as he tried to sit up.

"I...what did you...do to...where..." he coughed and stuttered.

"It is over, Rezzek," Aries said softly. He looked up at her, his eyes black as night.

"I am...not defeated yet...my love!" Rezzek forced himself to his feet, staggering a bit.

"Uhhhh, Aries?" Samantha stood herself and faced him from a distance.

Rezzek choked out a laugh and tried to walk forward, with little success. He raised a hand and made a fist, then opened it to reveal and small, black smoke twirled and danced in his hand. It was a pitiful display.

"I cannot...be defeated. I *will* not. Be defeated. *I am... death. I am...the bringer of...*"

Rezzek was cut off abruptly by an arrow piercing his chest. He looked down and choked. Out of thin air and several meters in the sky, Riku appeared with his sword above his head.

"Gooooooodddzillllla!" Riku shouted, coming down before Rezzek. He spun a full one hundred and eighty degrees, slicing his sword in a wide arc and coming to face Samantha. He clasped the sword in front of himself and bowed low, while behind him Rezzek's head fell neatly off his shoulders and he fell lifeless to the ground.

"What an entrance!" Calleigh shouted from every-where.

"Thank you, disembodied voice," Riku said, standing up straight. Behind him the body of Rezzek quickly turned to grey ash and blew away in the wind.

"Goodbye love," Aries whispered only loud enough for Samantha to hear. "May you find rest."

From his vantage point on Coit Tower, Apollyon could see clearly across the San Francisco Bay to the amassing military presence on Alcatraz Island. He stared intently, angrily, out at the fledgling assembly the humans had put together. It was hardly a fighting force at all, and almost made Apollyon sad for them. Almost.

He stood in one of the arches of the tower, and his anger trembled down from his person so strongly that cracks began to form in the concrete. His eyes grew darker as he watched the boats and helicopters from afar move around like little insects.

Apollyon glared even harder, he felt the Darkness from the other side of the country, a very part of himself, scream in terrible pain and then, be cleansed. He sniffed his nose, he could smell the putrid scent of rotting flesh, being purified. Even from where he stood now, he could tell that his servant Rezzek had failed for the last time.

"So," he said to himself, "you've found the Purifier, have you? This game just keeps getting more and more interesting. Well in that case..."

Apollyon cracked his neck, and suddenly Coit Tower exploded in a violent display. From the top down it was as though each grain of sand in the concrete ripped itself from one another. Debris and chunks of rock no bigger than a golf ball shot out in all directions. The explosion leveled the trees on Telegraph Hill and flattened nearby homes.

Yet, the Chaotic One floated in mid air, unflinching from his original position, his eyes still locked on the presence across the bay.

"Continue your work, Dark Ones. Lay waste to this miserable city. I have other pressing matters to attend to." Apollyon growled. He vanished from mid air as the wolf-like beasts howled their approval and continued to tear the city apart.

Page 107

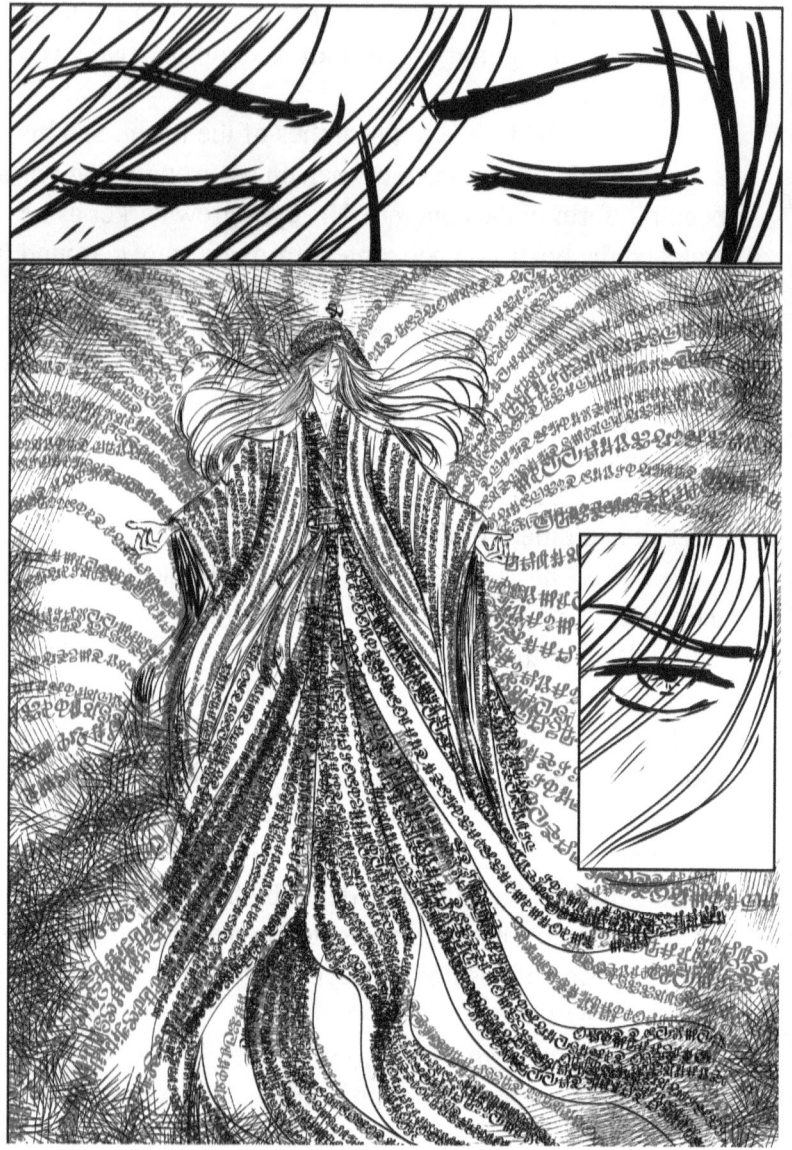

Mere moments later, Apollyon hovered a few meters off the ground over the remains of Paris, France. The destruction here was nearly complete, only one task remained. As if sensing his master's presence beforehand, the Wicked Man already knelt before Apollyon, awaiting orders.

"My master, how may I serve?" he said.

"The Zodiac are moving faster than I expected," Apollyon shouted from above. "Their stewards have already attempted an offensive. Weak though it was, I did not anticipate their strength to have advanced so quickly."

"Allow me to command the next attack, master. I will succeed where Rezzek has failed."

"Rezzek is dead, for good this time. He has been… cleansed."

The Wicked Man looked up suddenly at Apollyon. If he had had a real face, it would have worn a look of shock and sheer terror.

"The Purifier? So soon?"

"They cannot be allowed to gather the rest. Hit the next target before the Guardian is found. I refuse to let an age so… delicious as this one to go unsavored." Apollyon grinned as he looked around at the destruction. "Go. I'll awaken the other generals when I've finished here."

The Wicked Man bowed lower, his face almost to the ground.

"As you wish, master." He he pressed a bony palm to the ground and a dome of dirt and rock shot upwards and covered him. When the dirt fell back down the Wicked Man was gone.

Apollyon spread his arms out wide and raised himself up a little farther into the air. He laid his head back and closed his eyes as his robes opened and extended six times their original size. He grit his teeth and lifted his palms, the ground below trembled.

"Now," he hissed, "be forgotten!"

What structures that remained slowly began to sink in the vibrating earth beneath them. The catacombs caved in under the city and began to swallow up buildings and streets and rubble and all that was above them. The bodies of those murdered by the Dark Ones, those that hadn't already been burned or eaten, violently shook until even bone and marrow separated and became little more than dust among the rubble.

From all around Paris, millions of tiny streams of golden light snaked their way up into the air and towards Apollyon. One by one, they began writing in a language only known to the immortal beings, the names of those fallen in the Darkness. Apollyon breathed in the glory of his victory as he wiped away the very memory of the City of Light.

No more would Paris be remembered. History books would be rewritten, scholars would forget her very name, the art once housed in her museums would be known only to him. Wars, weddings, families and friends, all would be forgotten. Archeologists would one day discover long buried ruins and ponder the sudden destruction of such a place. But everything good and wonderful that Paris once stood for would be, from this day forward, forgotten.

After the attack in Brooklyn on Samantha, the stewards all decided it might be best to regroup in a safer environment.

There would be much to discuss, and Riku suggested they meet their newest member face to face.

"Ya don't really wanna come here, do ya?" Calleigh asked through the Cistern.

"Sure, why not? We're a team, right? We need to meet our newest teammate!" Riku shouted out to the air, though frozen in place.

"I was, uh, kind of in the middle of something," Jude protested, still in the wine cellar in Italy.

"Oh c'mon, Jude. I just nearly died. And we were all going to regroup after a bit anyway, remember?" Samantha said. "And besides, I *really* want to see the ancient city under a frozen volcano!"

"It's not half bad, if I do say so. Do you all have giant, supernatural hunky mentors, too?"

"Mine's a lady," Samantha smiled up at Aries.

"Mine's a, uh…Taurus is kind of emo," Jude answered looking away and speaking softly.

"You would talk," Taurus replied.

"You can hear me!?"

"I'm in the same room…"

The others laughed, which added a much lighter mood to the dark current situation. They all decided to meet in the City of Memory, and within moments, each steward and their accompanying Zodiac stood at the base of the grand staircase.

"No way!" Riku marveled at the massive underground civilization. "People lived here?!"

"Flourished here for quite some time," Sagittarius commented as he made eye contact with Aries. She nodded and nonchalantly headed off in a different direction.

"I believe you'll find the Purifier straight through there," Taurus pointed as Jude, Samantha and Riku headed off in that direction, like kids in a candy store.

Meanwhile, Taurus stole away into a separate abandoned structure where Leo, Aries, and Sagittarius were already waiting for him.

"I know this place," Taurus began, "yet I have no memory of it."

"Same here, I took Calleigh straight in, showed her the ropes and everything!" Leo blurted out. "But I'll be damned if I remember a thing! It's all kinda coming back, but hazy. Real hazy."

"This doesn't bode well at all," Aries added. "We are Timeless beings, we…we mimic the emotions of our charges but we do *not* truly experience them."

"Are you so certain of that?" Sagittarius turned to face Aries. She raised a finger in opposition.

"Once. *Once.* And never again. Besides he's dead, for good this time." She glared at Sagittarius.

"Never mind all that, there's something else all the brethren need to know." Leo rested a hand on Aries' shoulder and she lowered her glare. "As I sought the Purifier, I was approached by Aquarius."

"Aquarius has returned?" Taurus shouted.

"Yes, and he told me I needed to find the Cistern. Which we did. Here. *How* I found it I really don't know." Leo shook his head. "But he also told me it was never lost, but hidden. By him."

The others gasped as one hearing this news. Leo nodded fervently, his eyes lit up more like he was telling a ghost story around a camp fire.

"The Prophet. He met with someone in the woods. I felt a presence but the nature of the presence was hidden from me." Aries looked directly at Taurus.

"Yes. He has also discovered the true power within the tomes. Something very few Prophets have ever unlocked. If he met with Aquarius…" Taurus trailed off a moment.

"This explains nothing." Sagittarius growled as he removed his mask. "Why would Aquarius hide the Cistern? Why would he betray us and exile himself for so long?"

"Back in the vision of Atlantis, the Prophet summoned me, told me he had something to show me. That was the last age Aquarius partook in his charge with us."

"Could he have seen what drove Aquarius away?" Aries pressed.

"I do not know. But we may have to wait for answers. I can sense…" Taurus paused for a moment. "We need to get back with the stewards. The enemy moves."

The four unlikely stewards sat in what once was a great dining hall, eating sushi and laughing with each other about the absurdities that they all had faced over the last week. Calleigh drank in the stories with pure amazement as Riku reenacted everything from the fight atop Yggdrasil, to Jude getting tossed around the streets of San Francisco. The latter had Jude scowling, but Samantha comforted him with a hug, somewhat out of character for her, and more food.

"I forgot to ask," Calleigh began, "where all this sushi came from?"

"Oh, my friend Kazuha, her family runs a sushi restaurant just outside of Tokyo." Riku smiled.

"Ya went from New York, to Tokyo, for sushi?"

"Yeah. It's really good. Do you not like it?" Riku gave a look of concern.

"Oh aye, I just never thought I'd be eatin' take out sushi, *from* Japan, in an underground city in Antarctica."

They all laughed. Given the events of the past few days, it was something they desperately needed to do.

"Oh, so then Jude writes in his little book in his purse there," Samantha pointed to his satchel.

"It's a satchel, and it's a tome, thank you very much," Jude corrected.

"Right, satchel, tome, got it. Anyway, he has the power to change things. So he gave me this, angelic glow and voice…"

"No! Ya dinna make her really look like an angel?!" Calleigh said excitedly.

"He did, and the locals coming out of some church, oh my gosh, you should have seen their faces!"

Calleigh cupped her hands over her mouth in disbelief and gasped. "Ya know, when I asked my, uh…Leo, to show me a sign, he brought me the Pope!"

"Wait, the real Pope? From Rome?" Jude's eyes went wide as he turned his attention to Calleigh.

"Aye, he dinna speak a word of English and looked so confused, the poor man! 'Course then Leo blinked him right back or whatever he does."

"You're lucky," Riku said as he stuffed his mouth with more sushi. "When Sagittarius travels me around, he shoots an arrow. I get pulled along behind it like I'm being stretched by my neck!"

"Does it hurt?" Calleigh asked.

"No. Not at all. It's just really weird."

They all laughed. It was a good night.

Then Jude blinked.

He stood on top of a radio tower he had never seen before, but looked similar to the Eiffel Tower in Paris. He looked down at a city that was burning, he heard the blood curdling screams of thousands of people under attack by the Dark Ones.

Jude panicked, but he couldn't move to help them, he couldn't call for help, nor could he see his friends anywhere. Below him strode a tall figure in a dark, tattered cloak. As he walked, the ground rotted behind him, turning black and smoking as though it had been burning for days.

The cloaked figure suddenly looked up and made eye contact with Jude. He shot up from the ground like a rocket until he was face to face with Jude, his skeletal face inches from Jude's own. Jude couldn't move, just as before, but now felt petrified with fear.

Jude tried to look away but his head would not move, so he turned his eyes downward instead. In the distance he saw very clearly, as if it was right in front of him, a sign written in Japanese. The characters burned into his brain as the breath of the Wicked Man drew hot against his cheek. He felt his skin start to melt away on the side of his face, and he began to scream in pain.

"Jude!" Samantha shouted as she slapped him a second time. Jude came out of his vision, wide eyed and bewildered. He looked around frantically, Calleigh wore a look of terror; Samantha one of worry; and Riku…

"Riku!" Jude shot forward and grabbed Riku by the shirt, pulling him down to the table next to him. "This…what is this? Where is it?"

Jude pulled out his notebook and ripped away a sheet. He began writing, in perfect Japanese, the characters of Kanji and Hiragana he had seen on the sign.

"Where did you see this?" Riku asked.

"Never mind that! What is it? Where is it?"

Riku pointed at the characters and read. "It says 'Oda Sushi'. That's the name of my friend's restaurant. In Tokyo."

"They're coming. He's coming. The creature from Paris, from the catacombs."

"Jude, what are you talking about?" Samantha turned him towards her.

"Aye, you're freakin' me out," Calleigh said, taking a step back. Jude turned back to Riku and grabbed his shoulders with both hands.

"The Wicked Man. He's headed for Tokyo next."

"He's right," Taurus said as the Zodiac entered the room. "The Dark Ones are on the move."

Riku jumped from his seat, breathing hard and panicking.

"What do we do? We can't, they can't, not like San Francisco! Not like Paris!" He spun around and ran into Sagittarius, who grabbed him and lifted him straight off the ground.

"Warrior!" Riku stiffened. "Save. One. City." Riku grit his teeth and nodded.

"Sensei, I *will* do my best!" he said, just above a whisper. Sagittarius set him down gently and he turned to face the others. "Friends, time of rest is over. We have work to do."

Chapter 9

Riku was getting more and more accustomed to the strange mode of travel that Sagittarius used. This time, when landing on the outskirts of Tokyo, he actually caught the arrow before it struck ground. Moments later, it dissipated into nothing, but the fact remained that his reflexes, timing, and senses were all improving drastically with the constant practice.

His eyes darted all around from his position atop a small hill, but Riku didn't see any signs of the Dark Ones yet. He closed his eyes tight and recalled the conversation not long ago in the City of Memory with the other stewards and Zodiac as they discussed their plan of attack.

"If it's anything like San Francisco, we need to evacuate the city as quickly as possible," Samantha had said.

"That isn't so easy," Riku added. "If they attack all of Tokyo, that means upwards of thirty million people."

"You did just say *thirty*, is that right? Not *thirteen?*" Calleigh looked at Riku in disbelief.

"Yes. Tokyo is the largest city in the world. For our enemy to attack there, I don't think the four of us will be enough."

"We just need a plan, that's all." Jude said as he pulled his notebook out and stepped forward.

"I appreciate it, Jude, but this is not America. Japan is small and space is limited. We can't displace so many people so easily. And turning Samantha into an angel won't work."

Riku hung his head and sighed. "But I will not let my city fall and be forgotten forever…"

"Um, I know I'm the new one 'ere," all eyes turned to Calleigh who awkwardly had her hand raised. "But don't we have these immortal giants we can use, too?"

"Our power is limited in instances such as these," Sagittarius spoke up from behind his samurai mask. "We cannot directly interfere with the plans of Apollyon. That task is left to the stewards alone."

"Aye, but dinna ya tell me the big lady here burned one of their shamans or something to a crisp, twice?"

"We can assist," Aries answered, "but our involvement must be limited."

"But why? If this Destroyer or what not can do all this terrible stuff, why can't you?"

"We are bound by eternal guidelines," Taurus stepped forward. "Our charge is to find and train the stewards, but it is your responsibility to fight for and defend this world. We are teachers, we are seekers, but we do not fight *for* you."

The room was silent for a few minutes as they all contemplated their own fates and the revelation that they may be actually alone in all this. Finally, after a bit Riku spoke up again.

"Tokyo is my home, I won't see it burn. I know we can do something if we all act together. I only ask that we all do our best, then we will have victory."

The others didn't seem quite as convinced, but it was Samantha who stepped forward and put a hand on Riku's shoulder. Her gentle smile reminded Riku why she was chosen as the Healer.

"All right, your city, you call the shots on this one. Anyone disagree?" The other two shook their heads, even

Jude, surprisingly, had no qualms about letting Riku lead the charge.

After that, they all dispersed to different locations around the city, except for Calleigh who would run communications from her post with the Cistern. Unfortunately, none of the Zodiac had any memory of exactly how the Cistern worked, which was a problem that would need to be addressed later, but they knew that water was the key. So, Riku devised a plan that would take each member by various parks or fountains so that they could check in and coordinate with Calleigh as they went.

Now Riku looked around from his spot atop a skyscraper, overlooking the Chiyoda Ward, and noticed in the distance an unnatural mist rising up from Shinjuku Park. Normally he'd reach for his mobile phone, but lately things hadn't been working the way they used to. He pulled out a water bottle from his back pocket and stuck his thumb in the top.

"Okay, here goes," he whispered to himself. Nearby, a pigeon stopped in mid flight as it was about to land on the edge of the building. Riku smiled and breathed a sigh of relief.

"Hello again," Calleigh's voice came from all around him.

"Good to hear you, Purifier. Shinjuku Park shows activity. I'll head there, please let me know what you hear from the others."

"You got it, boss."

Riku pulled his thumb from the water bottle and the pigeon landed, giving him a look.

"Sensei, will you please?" Riku said as Sagittarius strode up behind him, mounted on his horse. He fired an arrow off and Riku drew his sword, ready for the fight to come.

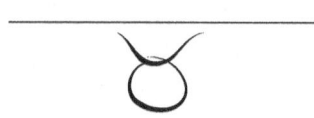

Jude was running reconnaissance on this mission, which, given his experience with Apollyon in San Francisco, he was very happy to do. He didn't have a sword like Riku, or a New York attitude like Samantha, or even a safe, hidden city to hide in like Calleigh. And while he would've rather been back in the memory of Atlantis, discovering the truth about Aquarius, the current situation did need all their attention instead.

Riku had placed Jude in the Bunkyo Ward, a residential and educational ward right on the edge of a beautiful park. Even though

he was on street level, Riku determined that Jude should be able to get an idea if any trouble started simply from the populace.

"They'll scream," Riku had said to him.

"You know I don't speak Japanese," Jude tried to warn him.

"Screaming is screaming in any language. They'll go, ahhhhh! And you'll know there's trouble."

Jude couldn't really argue with that logic. He patrolled the Koishikawa Park three times before deciding to get a little closer and check out the park grounds. He was immediately glad that he did the moment he stepped foot just outside the University Museum. A large cherry blossom tree sat quietly next to a beautiful large pond in a true picturesque environment. The blooms were light pink and white, and gave Jude the sensation that he had truly been whisked away to another world.

"Beautiful, isn't it?" Said an old Japanese man as he sidled up next to Jude. Jude was a bit shocked that the man spoke English, but he smiled back.

"Yeah, it…it really is something."

"Your first time in Japan?" The old man asked.

"Yes, it is. I've been doing a lot of travel lately. Didn't think I'd get a chance to come here, though."

The old man rested on a cane and smiled out over the pond, taking in the cool breeze and letting the silence speak for a few minutes. Jude fought the urge to speak and tried his best to simply be still and enjoy the moment. It wasn't easy coming from the high speed life he was used to, and especially now that apocalyptic events were occurring every few days. The old man sighed heavily and nodded his head at the pond.

"Japan has seen many hardships," the man started again, "but also many blessings. We make many mistakes, but we also pay our penance. It is good for foreigners to visit Japan. It is good to share what makes us Japanese."

Jude turned his eyes to the man, now curious more than simply being polite.

"What makes you Japanese?" He asked.

"That is what you come here to find out," the man turned to Jude and smiled. "But mostly good food." The old man grinned even wider and gave a slight bow to Jude. Jude wasn't sure how to respond so he bowed, quite awkwardly, in return.

Then the old man's face turned gaunt, his eyes rolled back into his head, and his hair melted away. Jude gasped as the man reached for him like one drowning in a pool, and screamed like a banshee. Jude couldn't move to help the man or to run away. The pond next to them boiled, and the cherry blossom tree burst into flames that danced and licked the air.

Jude's eyes shot around as he tried to take in everything he saw, though the very sight burned him and made him want to curl into a ball and hide. The old man's boney fingers now gripped his shoulder and pierced through Jude's shirt, slowly burying into his skin and drawing blood.

"Save...me!" The man gasped at Jude.

Jude heaved in a heavy breath and looked around, seeing the old man already several meters away, hobbling with his cane towards the other end of the park. Jude fell to his knees and thrust his hand into the pond, the water splashed but did not land as it hung in the air.

"Calleigh!" Jude tried to catch his breath. "Calleigh they're here."

"Oh aye, Riku just buzzed. He sees smoke rising over in the Shin...Shinju...Shin-something-or-other ward." Calleigh voice surrounded Jude.

"No, it's not there. It's the tower. Tokyo Tower. That's where it's starting." Jude panted.

"Oooohhhh my," Calleigh said softly.

"What is it?"

"That's...that's right where Samantha was headed."

Jude yanked his hand from the water and looked up to see Taurus was already towering over him. The Zodiac knelt down and drew close to Jude's face.

Page 124

"I do not expect you will simply stay here, then?" Taurus smiled.

"Damn right. What's that saying? The Pen is mightier than the sword?"

"That's a terrible saying," Taurus said, as he helped Jude to his feet. "Truly, Riku's sword would chop your pen right in half."

"Shut up," Jude shook his head. "Take me to Akihabara. I have an idea."

Samantha craned her neck and looked straight up the length of Tokyo Tower to the small circular cloud that formed at the top.

"Uh, Aries, tell me that's supposed to be there," she shielded her eyes from the glare of the sun and squinted to see.

"It is not, I'm afraid," Aries replied.

"Yeah, that's what I thought," Samantha quickly pulled out a bottle of water from her back pocket, removed the cap, and placed her palm on the nozzle. "Let's hope this works." She turned the bottle upside down, keeping the water from spilling out with her palm, but getting her skin wet just the same.

"Calleigh? Are you there?" The cloud stopped spinning and the sakura petals stopped flying in mid air. "Oh yeah, that's weird."

"Aye, I'm here!" Calleigh's voice rang out in Samantha's ears and all around her.

"Okay, we've got trouble at Tokyo Tower. I think this place is about to be ground zero."

"Tokyo Tower as well!?" Riku's said. "No no no! Samantha there's Shiba junior high and high school right north of where you are. You have to help them."

"Great, I'm on it. I'd much rather be there than here anyway. Where are you?"

"Shinjuku Park. Dark mist all over, I have to go." Riku's voice, and oddly his presence, vanished.

"Calleigh, have you heard from Jude?"

"Aye, he checked in a minute ago. He saw that cloud you're seein' now. He dinna say anythin' about comin' your way, though." Calleigh sounded nervous, and Samantha remembered this was her first real event as part of the team. She took a deep breath and nodded to herself.

"Okay, thank you Calleigh. Everything will be fine, so don't panic, and we'll keep checking in often. I'll go to that school, let Jude know I'm safe if you hear from him. Just... don't panic."

"Aye, I'm not panicking. Go do your thing, Healer."

Time caught up with Samantha, and she took a quick swig of water before launching into a job towards the school.

"I'm definitely panicking," Calleigh gasped, as she turned her worried eyes up at Leo, who wasn't helping by pacing the room. Leo stopped pacing and laughed.

"After you just told the Healer you weren't panicking? Ha!" Leo slapped his thigh and shook his head. "I love you humans."

"Oh give it a rest, will ya? You'll forgive me if I've never been charged with saving the world before. Or a city, for that matter!"

"Truly you're doing fine, Purifier," Leo moved closer and almost put his hands on the Cistern but stopped short. "The four of you will be able to stop this attack."

"Aye? Then why does it take twelve of us, and by what the others said, you've never been able to stop the big 'ol baddie, what's his name again, Apple yonder?"

"Apollyon," Leo scoffed. "Yes, he's always won, but only because we never had all the twelve artifacts...well, at least in several ages."

"Several ages? And what about the ages ya *did* have them all? Why dinna ya beat him then?"

Leo opened his mouth to answer but the words didn't come out. Why *didn't* the stewards win back then? If they had all twelve artifacts at one point in time, it stood to reason that they had a good fighting chance. So what happened in those instances? And why would this age be any different than ages past?

Suddenly Leo saw a very clear problem, he had questions. That was something a Zodiac should not, ever, have. They were eternal, Timeless Ones, fit with all the wisdom and knowledge of the galaxy as they needed to be. There was a blank space, though, there had to be. Otherwise what would be the point of questions pertaining to the past? And not just any random past, but a past in which he had partaken.

He looked up and saw Calleigh waiting for a reply, but he had none to give. Leo swallowed hard, he was actually a bit nervous, and that , more than anything else, frightened him.

"I…I need to go seek the answer to that question." He blurted out.

"What, now? You're leaving now?" Calleigh's demeanor changed, she raised one eyebrow and gave Leo a look that a husband might get after coming home late from drinking with his friends.

"I'll be right back. You'll be fine," Leo said, then with a pop and sudden gust of air, he was gone.

"I bloody better be fine or I'm kickin' your arse!" Calleigh shouted to the air. She turned her attention back to the Cistern and placed her hands on the edges. "Alright team, we can do this. We can do this. We can…" she paused and looked into the slowly spinning water. There was something inside the Cistern, reflecting the blue light from the room. No, two somethings.

Calleigh looked even closer, almost bringing her face into the water itself. Then she saw it, they were a pair of eyes looking back at her, but not at her, through her. In surprise, Calleigh pulled back and just as she did the eyes, the face, a whole person shot up through the water, without disturbing a drop, and burst from the Cistern.

Calleigh fell back on the floor as a man came up, dressed in a Greek style toga, with curly blonde hair and sandals, and grew larger as he emerged from the water. It all happened so fast, but by the time the man landed, he was as tall as Leo had been. He turned his kind face down to Calleigh and smiled, offering his hand.

Calleigh reluctantly took the help, and he pulled her fast to her feet.

"Whoa! Uh, hi there. Who might you be?" She asked, completely startled.

"I see Leo has left you alone? That is not very proper, but he never was one for propriety. Forgive my intrusion, but I was spying on the two of you just a tad bit. I am the Timeless Zodiac, Aquarius, The Water Bearer." Aquarius gave a curt bow, and then extended a hand.

"Oh, I see. I'm Calleigh, the red-haired wonder, the Purifier." Calleigh's face blushed to match her red hair as she took Aquarius' hand.

"A pleasure, truly. Now I hate to be hasty, but I believe you are in the middle of a skirmish, correct?"

"Oh, aye. Well, the others are. I'm just runnin' the radio here."

"Oh, but the Cistern is far more than a communication device. I'm certain you've discovered that by now. My dear Purifier, there is so much more, in fact, that you can do with this. I've come to help you understand."

"So you know a thing or two about it, then?" Calleigh was both charmed and intrigued.

"Goodness yes, my dear," Aquarius beamed. "You see, I created it."

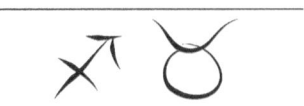

The moment Riku arrived at Shinjuku Park, he felt danger everywhere. The sun wasn't quite directly overhead, so each person, tree, and building cast a shadow. Each shadow became a portal for the enemy to enter into the area. As if the shadows themselves came to life, Dark Ones erupted out of the ground all around Riku, and immediately began tearing at trees, buildings, and people.

Riku didn't waste a single moment. He sprang into action, slicing his sword up and down and doing his best to draw the attention of the beasts as they emerged.

"Over here! I'm a steward! The Warrior! Come get me!" He waved one arm and shouted as the people nearby screamed and ran, if they could. For the most part, it worked; the Dark Ones would much rather have a chunk of flesh from a steward than just anybody. But he did notice strays escaping outside of the park. He cursed himself, but was too busy fighting off the ones nearby to give chase.

The training Sagittarius made him endure, facing off against multiple opponents, was coming in handy as he sliced through his enemy with little resistance. But, it was his endurance he began to worry about after only a few minutes of fighting.

Then Sagittarius came galloping onto the scene, firing his bow, arrow after arrow into the Dark Ones. Each hit was fatal, and quickly dispatched the beasts with a single blow. He rode in a wide path, striking at the ones that would escape to cause havoc elsewhere, while Riku focused on the interior of the park.

"They keep coming!" Riku shouted as his arms began to tire.

"This is but one ward," Sagittarius replied. "Soon the city will be overrun. You must think of evacuation."

"No!" Riku split another Dark One in half. "I won't let Tokyo end up like the other cities! I...can't!" He shouted, as he beheaded another. Fatigue was setting in fast, as he had never trained for long term combat. His fights in the kendo dojo were always over in a few seconds. But this was proving to be a task he might not be able to complete. And if he was stuck here, how would he fight around the rest of the city?

He thoughts betrayed him and slowed his reaction time, and Riku howled in pain as a razor sharp claw skimmed across his thigh. It was enough to bring him to his knees, and he had only enough time to look up and see the other claw coming to finish the job. Suddenly, a golden lance pierced the Dark One. It cried out in ungodly pain, and shattered into a cloud of soot.

Taurus, in full golden armor, stood on the other end of the vanquished foe. He offered the end of the lance, and Riku grabbed it and stood to his feet, wincing in pain.

"We came just in time, huh?" Jude smiled and patted Riku on the back.

"There's too many. I don't know how we can get them all," Riku tried to catch his breath, his head spinning a bit as well from the pain in his leg.

"Ouch, I can't do anything about that. But maybe if you catch up with Samantha," Jude dug into his back and pulled out his notebook.

"I...can't keep fighting...I need a...break."

"No you don't. Hey, you've heard of Gundum, right?"

Riku gave Jude a look.

"Everyone...in Japan has...heard of Gundum. There's a giant statue in...Akihabara." Riku panted.

Jude grinned. "I know." He turned his eyes down to his notebook and furious scribbled words, his eyes darting all over the page. Then he turned the notebook to Riku with a devious grin. In the center of the page was a decently drawn robot, commonly known as a "mech", and all around it words Riku couldn't read in English.

"Congratulations," Riku patted Jude on the shoulder, still not understanding what the Prophet was getting at. "Good drawing." Jude kept grinning, but backed away a few steps and watched Riku. He gasped as he felt his feet lift off the ground, and he slowly rose into the air.

"What!? What did you do?!" Riku looked frantically left and right as his body became encased in opaque mechanical gears and siding. Within moments, he found himself inside the exoskeleton of a four-meter tall, robotic mech suit. The Sword of Achilles even grew in size, and fit into the hand of the giant mech. Riku was ecstatic as he looked down at Jude.

"There! You'll run faster, hit harder, and be protected. The armor is something I made up in my head. It's not real, or, not from earth, I guess you'd say. The Dark Ones shouldn't be able to get through." Jude stood back and admired his handiwork.

"Thank you! Thank you so much!" Riku spun and swung the sword around. The suit responded to his every move, even his every thought, like it was merely an extension of him.

"Get going! I'll touch base with Calleigh and..." before Jude could finish Riku leapt into the air, soared over the trees at the border of the park and was gone. "Good. You got it. I'll just...yep."

Jude jotted a few things down in his notebook as Sagittarius galloped off after Riku, and Taurus came up beside him.

"You're getting good at that. Changing appearances."

"It's not an appearance. Technically it still *is* Riku, but a projection of his thoughts. That's why I needed to know if he'd seen a Gundum before. But yeah, thanks. I think I'm getting the hang of this...whatever I'm supposed to do." Jude smiled and stuffed his notebook back in his satchel.

"Good, then let us hurry to the next place you saw in your vision," Taurus readied his lance and looked on ahead, ready to move.

"Wait," Jude paused. "We can do this, right?"

"Do what?" Taurus asked without looking back.

"Ya know, save the world and all."

"The world? I do not know," Taurus said flatly, eliciting a frown from Jude. "But perhaps you should change my mind?" Taurus gave the faintest of smiles.

"I'll take that challenge," Jude smiled back. "Yes, you fight, I'll watch from a safe distance and not get killed," Jude took hold of Taurus' arm and off they went.

"Everyone out! Hurry please! Danger!" Samantha shouted everything she could think of that the young students might be able to understand. She immediately regretted not spending more time learning foreign languages, but even if she had, Japanese would probably not have been on the list. She peered out one window that overlooked Tokyo Tower, and could clearly make out the Dark Ones pouring from the cloud overhead. Samantha swallowed hard as another figure emerged from the cloud, larger and more human-like than the beasts.

"Lady?" Samantha looked down as a thin teenage girl tapped on her shoulder. "I speak some English. I can help," the girl said. Samantha turned and grabbed her by the shoulders.

"Wonderful. Get everyone away from the school, and away from Tokyo Tower. Get as far away as you can. Got it?" The young girl nodded. "Good, thank you!"

She turned from Samantha, and began shouting at her classmates with a certain degree of authority. Samantha looked back out the window to see the cloud now dissipated, but could make out screams coming from the distance.

Quickly, she grabbed her water bottle and turned it over on her hand. A student running by froze mid step.

"Calleigh! What's going on? Anything from Jude or…"

Suddenly, Calleigh stood in front of Samantha.

"Hello there! I'm gettin' a bit better at this, thanks to some help. Oh, Jude is on his way north, and Riku will be at your location in a moment. You should see him, though!"

"What do you mean I should see him?" Samantha looked outside the window, time was moving again, just not for her or her immediate surroundings. Just as she looked, she could swear there was a robot hanging off the side of Tokyo Tower.

"Uhhh, Calleigh? Is that…"

"Oh aye! That's him, alrigh'."

"Okay, I don't even want to know." Samantha shook her head. "As long as it's working…"

"Sam, look out!" Calleigh shouted and pointed down the hall. A Dark One slammed into a locker, quickly recovered, and came barreling down the hallway towards her. Samantha had seconds to react and saw no other choice but to jump through the window, but she was three stories up.

Calleigh jumped in front of her and thrust her arms up, though she turned her face away and cringed. The Dark One stopped dead, frozen in mid air, and snarled and whimpered.

It's human-like eyes went wide for a split second before it fell straight down to the floor into a withered husk. The corpse crumbled to ash before either of the women could react to what had just happened.

When Calleigh opened her eyes again, Samantha was staring at her, slack jawed.

"Come and get me! Come on!" Riku shouted as he leapt from the side of Tokyo Tower, spun, twisted, sliced a Dark One clean in half and landed on his feet. He was filled both with mirth and rage; mirth from the sheer fun he was having in a mech suit, and rage from his hometown being attacked by the enemy.

Yet, for every single creature he took down, and he was dispatching quite a few, Riku felt like four more took their place. And they were making progress, at least in a few of the wards. If this kept up, he didn't see how they would save the city at all. Not the four of them, at least.

"Hey, Warrior!" Riku spun to see a shimmering image of Calleigh, as though she was made of water. He noticed he could still move, though everything around him had slowed to an almost dead halt.

"Calleigh?" Riku squinted to try and focus, but it wasn't his eyes, she was definitely some kind of water projection.

"Aye, it's me. Somethin' big and strong came out of that cloud overhead a few minutes ago! Aquar...uh...my Zodiac friend 'ere said it might be worth lookin' into." Calleigh seemed to glance over her shoulder a moment, then resumed her smile towards Riku.

"Got it! Thank you!" Riku leapt without another word straight into the air and scanned the view below quickly while he hung for a few moments high in the sky. He spotted a lone figure in black robes, smoke trailing behind him, just as gravity took hold and pulled Riku back down. He made note of the location, and was upon the figure just after landing.

"You there!" He shouted, pointing his sword. Slowly, the Wicked Man turned towards Riku. He wore a bemused look on his face, and almost appeared to snarl.

"So, it's you that causes my master so much turmoil, is it?" The Wicked Man spoke slowly, as if chewing each word before vomiting them out.

"Uh, yes, it is I!" Riku posed, trying his best to appear menacing.

"I recognize your blade. It was last wielded by one of Rezzek's former comrades." He scoffed. "Little good it did that one. It will fare you no better."

"Is that all you have? Talk? Why not fight me yourself?" Riku challenged.

"Fool, all it took was a few words to distract you and seal your fate." Riku looked around him and noticed what appeared to be a small army of Dark Ones surrounding him on all sides except right in front. The Wicked Man must have conjured them there while Riku was focused on him.

"Now you're surrounded. No way to escape. Goodbye, little Warrior." The Wicked Man laughed.

Riku gripped his sword with both hands and smiled back.

"Not surrounded. I don't need to escape. You do." Riku shot forward with enough force to crack the concrete he stood on. The Wicked Man was right about one thing, the only way out was forward. His eyes widened in surprise as Riku's mech crashed into his skeletal body, and the two of them flew a hundred meters down the street.

Riku planted his feet to stop while the Wicked Man was flung farther still, tumbling and crashing into a parked car another dozen meters down the road. He didn't stop, but charged forward again, even as he heard the growling of the pursuing Dark Ones behind him. The Wicked Man barely got to his feet before Riku crashed into him, his sword at the Wicked Man's throat.

"Tokyo is my city!" The two crashed into a pillar. "Japan is mine to protect!" Riku grabbed his enemy's entire head in his large hand and started smashing it against the asphalt. He raised the sword up with his free hand, ready to impale the Wicked Man.

The creature's eyes were wide with fear, he cast a black bolt of power against Riku, knocking him off. Riku hit the ground on his back, and could see the man-beasts about to catch up with him. He glanced at a fire hydrant and struck it quickly.

"Calleigh!" He cried out. The water poured out, and the shimmering image of the Purifier came forward as well.

"No," the Wicked Man said in a very desperate and matter of fact manner.

Calleigh shouted something unintelligible, and thrust her arms out to both sides. A shockwave emanated out from her that vaporized some of the gushing water from the hydrant. A torrent of mist went out in all directions, disintegrating every Dark One it touched.

The mist continued out wider and wider so long as Calleigh held her shout and kept her arms raised. Riku sat up and watched in amazement. Then she dropped her arms, fell to her knees, and the image of Calleigh vanished.

Riku turned his attention to the Wicked Man, who was starting to rise. There was burned flesh that hissed and sizzled all over his body and face. He looked ragged and exhausted as he faced Riku.

"You cannot...defeat us," he wheezed. "We are immortal...you are...only human."

Riku stood up and raised his sword as if to strike his enemy down. In an instant, the Wicked Man snapped his boney fingers and disappeared from sight. The giant mech suit also began to fade and crumble, gently lowering Riku to his feet.

As he touched down, Sagittarius strode up from around a corner, nodding his approval.

"Well done, Warrior. Well done! We have rounded up the stragglers, but the day is yours. The city is safe." Sagittarius said, his eyes burning bright, and his smile beaming even from behind the mask.

"I couldn't have done it better myself," Jude added as he and Taurus, now back to his normal look, walked up as well.

"No, we did this. The four of us together." Riku had to reach up to put his arm around Jude's shoulder. "Samantha? Is she okay?"

"She's still at the school, tending to any wounded," Taurus replied. "She's fine."

Sagittarius looked up into the sky, beyond the skyscrapers of Tokyo. The others looked up as well, all staring into the partly cloudy blue Japanese sky.

"What are we looking at?" Riku whispered to Jude.

"I have no idea," Jude answered back.

Sagittarius turned to Taurus and rested a hand on his shoulder.

"They're coming, brother," he said sternly.

"Who? Who's coming?" Riku looked back and forth between the two Zodiac.

"Gemini, the Twins," Sagittarius burst into laughter. Taurus looked deflated as he sighed.

"Great. Let's get going," he muttered as he turned from the rest and headed back towards the school. The other three in tow, Sagittarius laid back on his horse, his laughter carrying throughout the city.

Epilogue

In a quiet nursing home in Kyoto, Japan, lay an old man, nearly forgotten entirely, save for his twice daily check ups and bed changes. His chart read "Nanashi-no-Gombee", roughly translated to "nameless" or "anonymous", since he arrived several years ago unconscious, and hadn't yet awakened from an extended coma.

Nevertheless, a wealthy widow from Osaka had caught wind of his situation, and made arrangements for his care so long as it was needed. Even when she too had passed away, the trust she had established in his name continued to provide for care. So there he lay, day after day, in a somewhat peaceful sleep.

As the nurse left the room to watch the news of a terror attack in Tokyo, two child-like figures hopped into the room and began to giggle amongst themselves. They both stood about a meter and a half, and were nearly identical except one was male and the other female. "Brother and sister" may have been a better description of the two. They approached the nameless old man in his bed, and eyed him with a look that bordered on reverence.

"He'll be relieved to be awake..." began the boy.

"But shocked to learn how much time has passed," finished the girl.

"Time is meaningless, though. He'll understand that timing..."

"...is everything. After all, he entered his sleep with a sense of..."

"...purpose. Now it's purpose that wakes him up!"

The two both smiled down at the man, then looked up in unison to catch one another's eyes.

"What fun this will be," began the girl. "We haven't seen big brother Taurus since..."

"...the last age. It seems like forever since we've swung on his horns. I wonder if he'll..."

"...tell us a story of his adventures thus far with the Prophet?! We do love his stories, don't we brother?"

"Yes we do, sister." The boy smiled and reached for his belt, where a rapier suddenly materialized. He drew the thin blade from it's sheath, as the sister drew hers. They crossed blades over the sleeping man, though not touching, and for the first time since their appearance, spoke in unison.

"Guardian, we Gemini, The Timeless Zodiac, The Twins, rouse you from your sleep." The two both backed off their blades, then struck them together, creating a small shockwave as they both shouted.

"Wake up!" They yelled.

A moment passed, then the old Japanese man opened his eyes.

To Be Continued in

The Timeless Zodiac
Book III

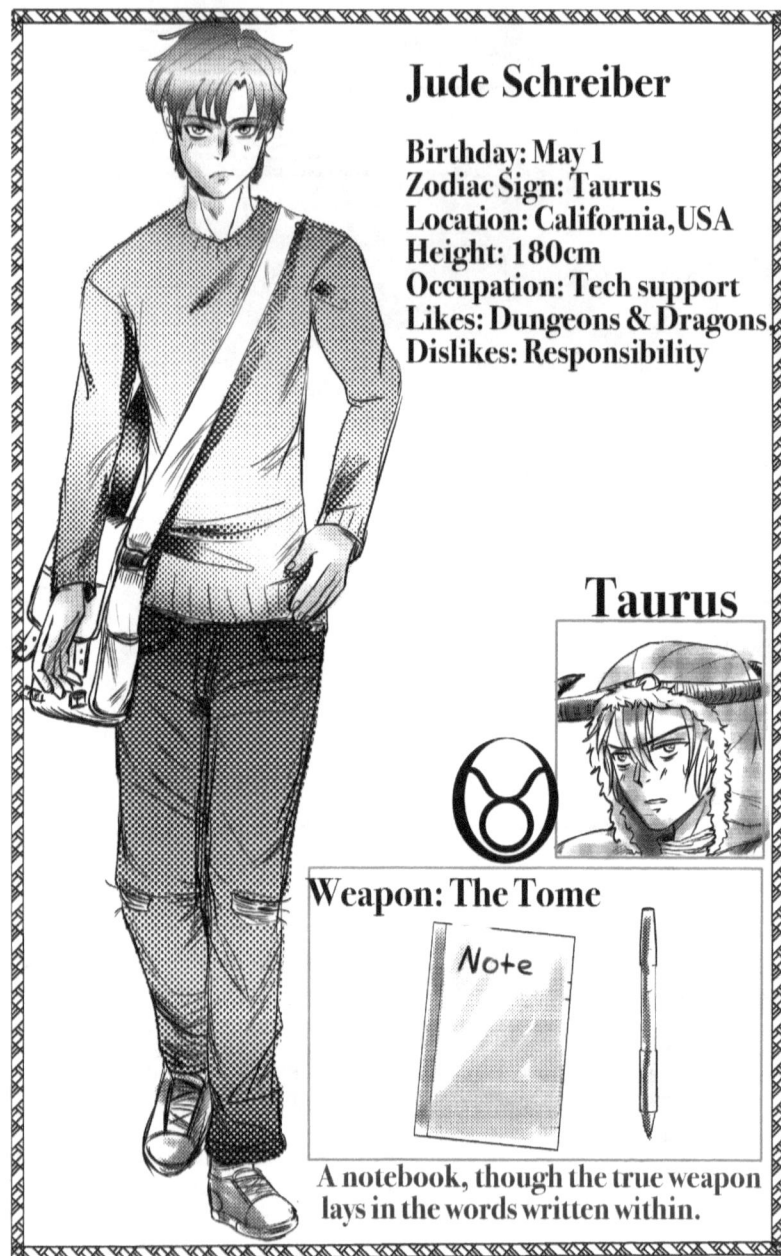

Jude Schreiber

Birthday: May 1
Zodiac Sign: Taurus
Location: California, USA
Height: 180cm
Occupation: Tech support
Likes: Dungeons & Dragons
Dislikes: Responsibility

Taurus

Weapon: The Tome

Note

A notebook, though the true weapon lays in the words written within.

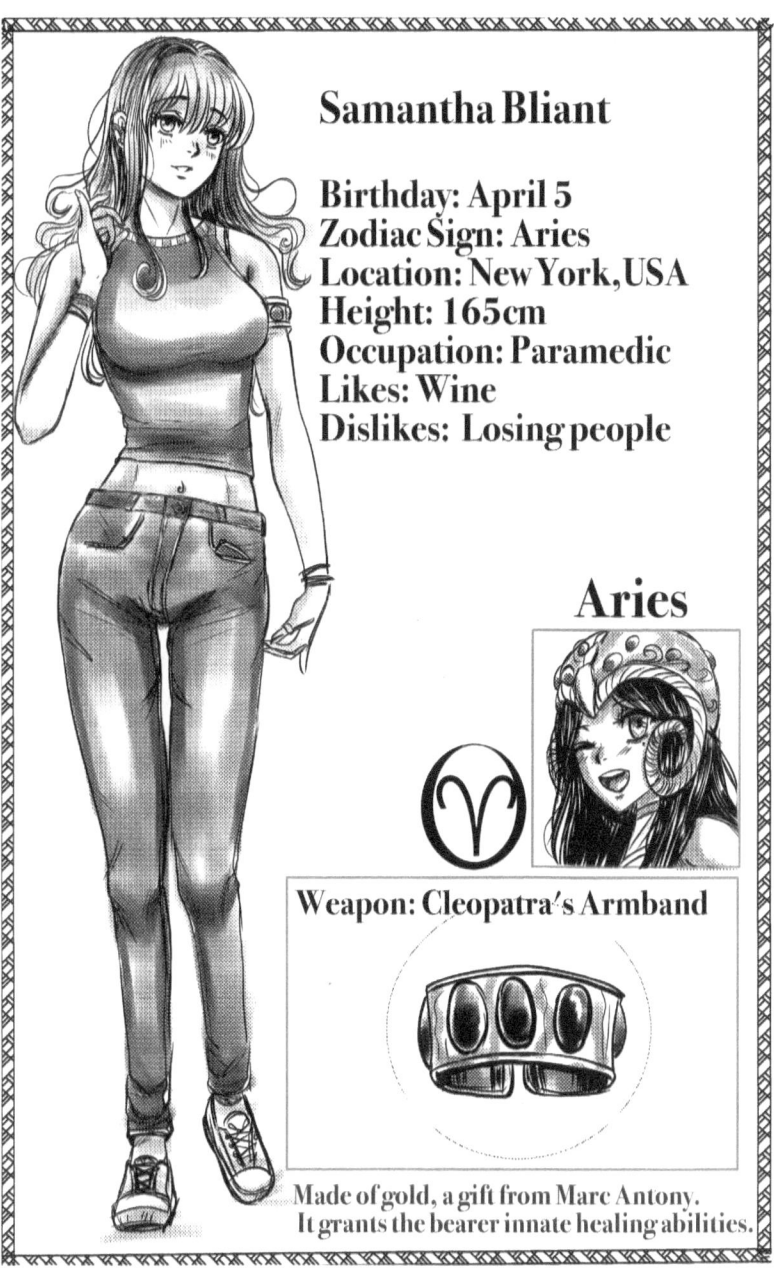

Samantha Bliant

Birthday: April 5
Zodiac Sign: Aries
Location: New York, USA
Height: 165cm
Occupation: Paramedic
Likes: Wine
Dislikes: Losing people

Aries

Weapon: Cleopatra's Armband

Made of gold, a gift from Marc Antony.
It grants the bearer innate healing abilities.

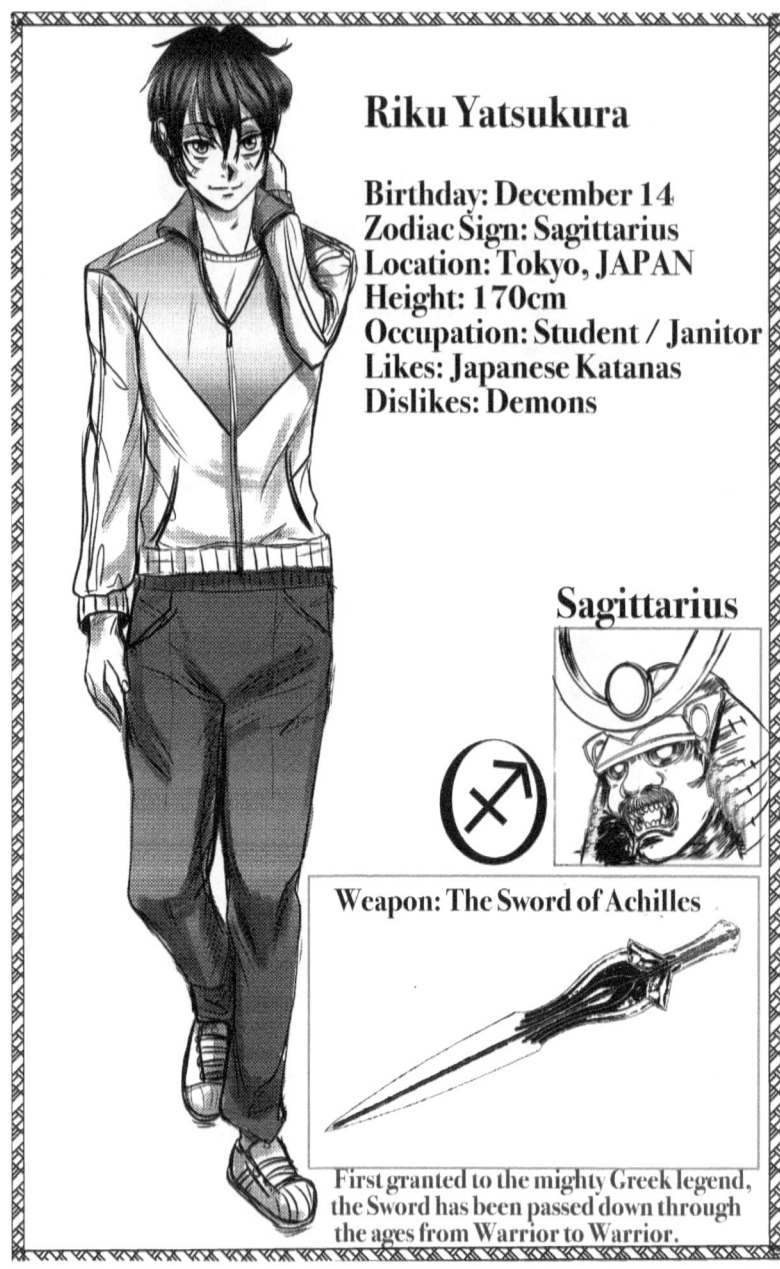

Riku Yatsukura

**Birthday: December 14
Zodiac Sign: Sagittarius
Location: Tokyo, JAPAN
Height: 170cm
Occupation: Student / Janitor
Likes: Japanese Katanas
Dislikes: Demons**

Sagittarius

Weapon: The Sword of Achilles

First granted to the mighty Greek legend, the Sword has been passed down through the ages from Warrior to Warrior.

Calleigh Morrison

Birthday: July 27
Zodiac Sign: Leo
Location: Hammerfest, Norway
Height: 157cm
Occupation: Archaeologist
Likes: Romance Novels
Dislikes: Pushy men

Leo

Weapon: The Cistern

Lost to time, the cistern grants the Purifier power over time and space itself.